MAN VS. GRIZZLY

"When Barney gets done with you, Manning," Rawlins said, "Laura Engle won't even look at you.

"Get it over with, Barney. If you don't, maybe I'll have to do the job myself."

"The hell you will," Burris snarled, and drove at Mark, his great arms extended as if he intended to hug his enemy to death.

Mark was afraid, as afraid as he'd ever been. He knew how Burris fought, he knew the man intended to kill him, or maim him for life, so he would be better off dead than alive, and he knew Burris had the physical strength to do it. Then Burris was rushing at him, and after that everything he did was prompted by the basic instinct of survival. . . .

Other Avon Books by
Wayne Overholser

RED IS THE VALLEY

Coming Soon

PROUD JOURNEY

Wayne Overholser

LAND OF PROMISES

AVON BOOKS ◆ NEW YORK

All of the characters in this book are fictitious, and any resemblance to actual persons, living or dead, is purely coincidental.

AVON BOOKS
A division of
The Hearst Corporation
105 Madison Avenue
New York, New York 10016

Copyright © 1962 by Doubleday & Company, Inc.
Published by arrangement with John K. Payne Literary Agency, Inc.
Library of Congress Catalog Card Number: 88-92126
ISBN: 0-380-70679-2

First Avon Books Printing: March 1989

AVON TRADEMARK REG. U.S. PAT. OFF. AND IN OTHER COUNTRIES, MARCA REGISTRADA, HECHO EN U.S.A.

Printed in the U.S.A.

K–R   10   9   8   7   6   5   4   3   2   1

Part 1

The Camps
on the Gunnison

1

Mark Manning

1

When Mark Manning was a small boy, his father read to him from the Bible and *Gulliver's Travels* and a book of ancient Greek and Roman myths. He talked to Mark as if he were a man, and Mark listened, even though he did not understand all of it. Later, when he was grown, Mark remembered much of what his father had said about God and man's relationship to Him and to himself. Most of all Mark remembered his father's question: Why do men do the things they do to each other?

When Mark was a boy, he thought this must be the Great Question, for he heard his father ask it so often, but he never received an answer. Later, when Mark was grown, he asked many questions. His father's question was always among them. He could not have been his father's son, without asking that question.

2

Most of the hard miles were behind Mark Manning. On this day, August 14, 1881, he was not far from the end of the trail. Riding his buckskin gelding and leading his pack horse, he had left Pueblo a week before. He had come up the Arkansas to Canon City, had swung around the Gorge and had come to the river again, climbed over Marshal Pass and had ridden down the Tumitchi to the town of Gunnison.

Now the town, too, was behind him. He had followed the Gunnison River for a time, had forded it, and then had continued along the south bank. When he glanced at the sun, he decided it was time he found a camping place.

3

There were not many hours of sunlight left and most of the desirable sites were taken. Perhaps he had waited too long.

Mark had ridden through this country four years ago when he had quit his job at the Los Piños Agency on the Uncompahgre River some seventy miles to the west. At that time the Gunnison Valley had been an almost empty land. Today he found it hard to believe what he was seeing. From the moment he had left the town of Gunnison he had passed camp after camp: covered wagons, tents, and men with saddle horses and pack animals who, feeling no need for shelter, were living in the open anywhere they could squeeze into a spot along the river.

It was no secret, of course, that the Ute reservation would soon be open for settlement. The news had been printed in almost every newspaper in the state. Still, Mark had not expected to see so many people who were willing to leave jobs and friends and homes to find new ones.

The camps were strung out ahead of him as far as he could see. There were five or six hundred people here at least, he guessed, and more would come. He wondered wryly if there was enough good land on the reservation to satisfy all of them.

He shook his head, knowing that many of these people would fail. Hope had compelled them to come, hope and the dream that life would be better on the other side of Blue Mesa and Cerro where the Uncompahgre curled toward the northwest. It would have to be better, they would say. How could it be any worse?

The Promised Land was beckoning again just as it had beckoned from the day the Israelites invaded the land of Canaan. Or perhaps long before when the first cave man was lured from his home by a tale of better and roomier caves beyond the horizon.

Mark rode slowly, thinking of this as he watched children run through the grass and heard them shout to one another. He saw fishermen wading the stream, women kneeling along the bank to wash clothes, swimmers splashing in the deep pools, men playing cards on a blanket spread on the grass. Every one of them had a dream, Mark thought, and the rosier the dream, the greater their disillusionment would be when they saw the arid, adobe land that lay north of the Uncompahgre. Some would turn back then, for such a dream was too beautiful, too light, and far too fragile to withstand the jarring impact of reality.

For every man and woman, and perhaps every child old enough to dream his own dream, the Promised Land was different. No, Mark decided. Not the Promised Land, but the Land of Promises. For each and every one who dreamed his dream the promise would be what he wanted it to be, for these people were the weavers of dreams.

Not one of them, Mark told himself, would give a thought to the Utes who were losing the land of their fathers. But he was no better. Sure, he sympathized with the Indians, but he would take his share of the land along with the others.

He argued with himself as he had many times. The taking of land had always been a necessary part of the settlement of the West. It had been that way from the very beginning; it was the way it had to be. Some men could face the hardships and privations of the frontier and survive. He was such a man, a man who could help tame a wild land so other, weaker men could come later and find homes beside his.

He shook his head, his temper turning brittle as he stared ahead at the columns of smoke rising from the cook fires along the river. He was rationalizing and he knew it, and suddenly without conscious direction his thoughts rushed back across the years to his father who had asked the Great Question.

3

Mark Manning was born March 21, 1852, in a small community in Missouri not far from St. Louis. The hour was 5 A.M. on a windy, rain-drenched morning. His mother smiled through her tears at his father, for she had heard the doctor say it was a boy. She whispered, "Love him, George. Love him for both of us." Five minutes later she was dead.

When Mark was older, his father said, "We buried your mother on a clear, windy day. The rain had stopped. I was glad of that. I was glad for the wind, too. It seemed to me it was blowing your mother's spirit to whatever level of Heaven she was destined to go. It would be the top level. That was the kind of woman she was.''

He paused, and then he said thoughtfully, "I think she knew she was going to leave me. I wish I had known.''

Mark nodded, looking very solemn, for he sensed the seriousness of the moment and the depth of feeling that was in his father, but he did not understand. Afterward he thought about it many times, but it was not until he was grown that he realized how much his father had loved his mother and how much he had missed her and why he had never married again or never so much as looked at another woman. When he was old enough to understand, he marveled that his father had loved him enough for two parents, that never by word or gesture had his father shown any bitterness toward him for being the cause of his mother's death.

George Manning was a storekeeper, a small man with a big hatred of slavery. This was not a healthy attitude in that part of Missouri. Besides, there were nosey women in the community who felt he was not doing right by young Mark. For a time when Mark was a baby his father had hired a housekeeper, but he was not a wealthy man and he let her go as soon as Mark was old enough to take care of himself.

The sheer emergencies of daily life developed independence and self-reliance in Mark, and that was the way his father wanted it. In later years when Mark thought about it, he wondered if his father found a woman's presence in the house so painful that it was easier to do the housework and run the store himself than to have a woman around and be forced to talk to her. Even when he was a small boy Mark noticed that his father was always at ease with men, but he was shy with women, and when one came into the store, he was stiff and overly courteous.

Perhaps it was the widows in town who, having found George Manning unapproachable, started the talk about Mark being neglected, and perhaps it was this vicious gossip more than his views about slavery which led him to sell out in the summer of 1859 and go to Colorado to search for gold.

Mark was seven that summer, young enough to enjoy the adventure and old enough to be of some help to his father. While the men in the party cursed the heat and the dust and the thunderstorms and the Indian danger which never quite materialized, Mark had a wonderful time.

They met the first Gobacks on the trail. Wagons that had rolled west a few months before with the letters on the canvas, PIKES PEAK OR BUST, now had a line drawn through the words. Below was a new sign, BUSTED BY GOD. Sometimes a third sentiment was added, GOING BACK TO AMERICA. George Manning knew long before he reached Denver that the bubble had burst and he recognized the myth for what it was, knew that he would not pick up nuggets of gold on the banks of Cherry Creek, but the luster of adventure was not tarnished for young Mark.

When they caught the first glimpse of the Continental Divide, its white peaks mixed with the clouds so it was hard to know which was which, Mark simply stood and stared and felt a thrill such as he had never felt before. He would never be a Goback; this was where he belonged, and someday he would climb those peaks, maybe even live up there in the snow above the clouds.

The winter in Denver was hard. Prices were high: eggs two dollars a dozen and apples fifty cents apiece if you could find any. What was even worse was the scarcity of work. George Manning's money was disappearing at an alarming rate. Storekeeping was all he knew. He was neither big nor strong, and the inordinate amount of violence frightened him.

He was afraid to be out on the streets after dark, so he stayed with Mark in the evenings and talked to him and told him stories and read to him from the few books he had brought with him. He had owned a large library in Missouri, but he had sold nearly all of his books.

George Manning was not a church-going man, but he was reverent, and in later years whenever Mark thought about his boyhood, it always seemed to him that his father had had no fear of death and that he had a greater understanding of God than any other man he had ever met.

His notion of God was not of ritual and dogma, not a

God who was pleased by the making of images and incense burning and the offering of sacrifices, but a God for living men, a God of beauty, a God who made rain and snow and wind, a God who made things grow in the spring and die in the fall and be born again in the spring, a God of love.

"Too few people have any capacity for love," Mark's father said. "They think they do and they go through the forms of it, but that's all. I believe that God wants us to learn to love more than anything else. And another thing. The evil and the ugliness you see all around you are made by man, not God."

He paused and thoughtfully filled his pipe, and then he said, "I think I understand more than most people do. Most of it has come to me since your mother died, and I often wonder if somehow she has found a way to tell me what she knows, but there is one question I cannot answer at all. Why do men do the things they do to each other?"

And Mark, staring at his father's troubled face, was surprised that there was something his father did not know.

In the spring George Manning had enough money left to buy supplies to fill his wagon. With Mark sitting on the seat beside him, he drove up Clear Creek to the diggings and built a two-room cabin, the front room for the store, the back room their sleeping quarters, kitchen, and parlor. He spread sawdust on the dirt floor and covered it with a gunnysack carpet which he pegged down at the corners and along the sides. He built a counter and a few shelves and was open for business.

The miners liked him and there were few women on Clear Creek to bother him. He prospered and soon had to return to Denver to buy supplies. He and Mark remained on Clear Creek that winter. In the spring he sold out and moved up to Blackhawk. Again he started a store and again he prospered.

But for Mark's father prosperity was not the answer. He was restless, and as the news of the fighting in the East trickled into Blackhawk, his restlessness grew. His conscience bothered him because he, George Manning, had hated slavery all his life and yet he was doing nothing about it.

He wanted to join the Colorado Volunteers but there was no one with whom he could leave Mark. This was something else Mark did not understand until years later.

In the summer of 1863 they moved again, this time to a small camp named Achilles which had sprung up around a new strike above Central City. George Manning hated big camps. They were ugly and filthy and stunk with the smell of man, he told Mark.

People threw their garbage into the street. Butchers let their offal rot on the ground beside their shops. Freighters made no effort to clean up after their horses and mules. All of it added up to more than a man could stand, Mark's father said.

Achilles really wasn't much better except that there were fewer people, and that in itself, George Manning said, was an improvement. The wind seemed to blow continually up here, and there was almost no summer at all. Mark discovered that he could find snow nearly any time of the year if he searched in the deep gullies on the north sides of the mountains which were protected from the sun.

Now, Mark told himself, he was living where he had said he wanted to live when he had first seen the mountains, in the snow among the clouds. Often he actually was among the clouds when they settled down upon the camp, or when the summer storms blotted out the sun. He could not even see the nearby peaks when lightning snapped at the earth and thunder rumbled across the sky and shook the earth with its passing. It was awesome and frightening to Mark, yet he would not have missed it for the world.

The end of life as he had known it for twelve years came suddenly and violently and without warning in the summer of 1864. Mark was in the back room opening crates of canned goods when he heard men talking to his father in the store. Something was wrong. He wasn't sure how he knew, but he knew. Perhaps it was the ominously threatening tone of their voices.

He slipped to the door and peeked around the casing and almost cried out in shock. Two men had pistols in their hands and were holding up his father who was scraping money out of a drawer into a canvas sack.

Mark knew his father had a loaded revolver under the counter, but he wouldn't be able to get it. There was also a loaded rifle in the corner behind Mark. He had used it many times in the year they had lived here, sometimes just for target practice with his father, and sometimes for hunting.

Mark eased back from the door, slipped across the room to where the rifle leaned against the wall, cocked it, and returned to the door. He wasn't sure what he could do, but he'd do something. He started to slide the barrel of the rifle around the casing, thinking that he'd yell at them to throw their hands up, but before he had six inches of the rifle barrel past the casing, he heard a pistol shot.

Mark's heart bounced into his throat. One of the men said, "That'll shut his God-damned mouth." When Mark looked he saw that his father was draped across the counter, and that the outlaws were walking through the front door, one of them carrying the sack of money. He shot one of them in the back, the bullet going between the shoulder blades. The other one bolted for his horse, not even bothering to pick up the sack of money that the man Mark shot had dropped.

Mark ran to his father and tried to turn him over but he couldn't. Someone else was shooting in the street, then men ran into the store. One of them said, "We got the son of a bitch, Mark. Delaney shot the top of his head off."

Mark didn't hear. He was staring at his father's motionless body; he saw the men ease him to the floor. One of them felt for his pulse and shook his head. Mark didn't cry then. He didn't cry until he was in bed that night, alone in the room back of the store.

He heard the wind scream around the corners of the building and he thought that tomorrow they would bury his father who had been both father and mother to him for twelve years. Then he remembered the question his father had raised. Why do men do the things they do to each other? That was when Mark began to cry, and he wondered if his father knew the answer now.

4

Before Mark found a camping place beside the Gunnison River, he met a man who might have stepped out of the pages of the Old Testament. He was as tall as Mark or taller, well over six feet with the wide shoulders and muscular arms of a blacksmith. He carried a heavy pack on his back and a staff in his right hand that was as big around as Mark's wrist.

Mark had seen more than fifty men since he had forded the river and turned west along its south bank, but they had been the usual land seekers, run-of-the-mill men who had probably found it easier to pull up stakes and seek a new life than to continue with the old. But this man had been cast in quite a different mold.

He was about sixty, Mark judged. His clothes were old and worn, but they were clean. His face stirred Mark's interest and gave him the thought that the man might be a modern Moses who could strike a rock with his staff and bring forth a stream of water.

His full white beard was at least a foot long. The skin of his face that was not covered by his beard had been darkened by wind and sun until it was the color of old leather; his nose was as sharp as a saber. When he tipped his head back to look at Mark, his dark eyes had a penetrating quality that seemed to bore into a man and lay his soul bare. Moses, Mark thought, or Elijah, or possibly John the Baptist.

Mark nodded and said, "Good afternoon."

The old man raised his left hand in greeting. "May the Lord show you a shining face."

Mark rode on, afraid the old man would try to convert him on the spot, but he stopped reluctantly when the man called, "Friend."

Mark glanced back. The old man said, "My name is John Draper. I judge you are a land seeker."

"You could call me that," Mark said, "although the Utes would say I was a land thief the same as the others who are camped along the river."

"I understand why they would feel that way," Draper said, "but they forget that there was a day when they took the land from some weaker people. If we let ourselves grow weak, there will come a day when a stronger people will take it from us. That is the story of man."

Mark nodded, not wanting to argue. He knew some of the Ute legends, knew that they believed Keeche Manitou had given them the mountains because they were brave and had permitted other less favored tribes to live on the plains which were more undesirable than the mountains. But bravery had not been enough to hold the Ute homeland against the political and military power of the United States.

Mark would have ridden on if Draper had not asked. "You are looking for a campsite where there will be grass for your horses and wood for your fire?"

"I sure am," Mark said, "but looks like I'll have to go to the Lake Fork to find it."

"No," Draper said. "You will find what you seek about one hundred yards downstream. There is a good spot just beyond Will Engle's wagons where a family camped for two weeks. They left this morning. It was the tragic story of a weak man who could not turn his back on the temptations of the gaming table. He lost everything, so they had to return to their former home."

"Thank you," Mark said.

As he turned his head, Draper said, "There will be religious services Sunday morning and afternoon about fifty yards upstream under those cottonwoods you just passed. The river bottom slopes gently there. We will have baptismal services if my preaching is blessed and souls are saved. You will be welcome, friend."

This time Mark did ride on, not looking again at the old man who leaned on his staff staring at Mark's back, his dark eyes speculative.

Funny, Mark thought, how many men had tried to save his soul in the seventeen years since his father had died. He didn't know about Draper. He might be honest and sincere, even dedicated, but his God would be the Jehovah of the Old Testament, not the God Mark's father had believed in. The strange part of it was that most of the men who had tried to save Mark's soul were men who would do well to worry about their own.

He rode past a wagon and two sleek bays that were staked out in the knee-high grass south of the road. A slender, sweet-faced girl about twenty was bending over the cook fire. She straightened as Mark came opposite her and smiled. He touched the brim of his hat to her, his gaze moving past her to a big-bottomed, heavy-breasted woman who was wearing a man's pants, shirt, and hat.

The woman was chopping a limb off a deadfall cotton-wood, her ax strokes as powerful and true as a man's would have been. She stopped and turned, perhaps sensing Mark's presence. She wiped a sleeve across her sweaty forehead and scowled, and gestured for Mark to ride on.

The girl at the cook fire gave him her back and bent over the flames again. Queer, he thought. A friendly girl and an unfriendly woman. Mark had not seen a man around the wagon. He wondered if the women had a man, or if they had come this far without one. The big woman looked capable. Probably they were self-sufficient and a man would be unnecessary baggage.

Mark found the place the preacher had mentioned. Two wagons side by side, a tent between them and the river, the horses staked across the road and ample space for a camp just beyond. A girl was with this outfit, too. She was about the same age as the first one, but larger and stronger looking. Her eyes rested briefly on him, then she turned to the fire to look at the supper that was cooking there. She seemed neither friendly nor unfriendly, he thought. Just indifferent.

Two men were with the outfit. One, his back to Mark, was squatting by the fire poking it with a stick. The other, an old man with a skimpy beard, had waded into the river and was tugging at some driftwood which had lodged against a big rock.

Mark reined into the vacant area beyond the two wagons and dismounted. A party had been here, all right, judging by the refuse and the tramped-down grass. There was more than room for one man and two horses. The next camp was fifty yards or more down the river, partially hidden behind a thicket of willows.

As Mark stripped gear from the horses and watered them, he glanced at his neighbors' camp, wondering about them. In contrast with the weathered appearance of the other outfits he had seen along the river, the two wagons and the tent still had the shine of newness upon them. They had been bought only a few weeks ago, Mark judged, probably for this very purpose. Greenhorns, he decided, right out of Denver or Pueblo or some other city.

Mark staked out his horses and was returning to where he had left his gear when the man who had been squatting beside the fire said something to the girl and wheeled and strode toward him. He was about forty, with black brows and a spade beard. He was less than average height, so he had to cock his head back to look at Mark's face. His hair had receded, making his forehead seem inordinately high. He had a pompous manner that instantly grated on Mark's nerves.

The man held out his hand when he reached Mark. He said, "The name's Will Engle."

"Mark Manning."

They shook hands, Engle asking, "Just get in?"

"That's right."

"I was thinking I might need this grass," Engle said tentatively. "I've got two wagons and they're pretty heavy. When they give us the word, I sure want my horses to be in good shape. They say there's a heavy grade over Blue Mesa and another one afore you hit Cedar Creek."

"You own this grass maybe?" Mark asked. "And the land, too?"

"Hell no. You know I don't."

"Maybe you figured on throwing me off?"

Engle stepped back and scratched his bald spot. His eyes swept Mark's long, muscular body, noting the pistol that he carried on his right thigh, and made a sickly try for a smile. "No, I sure didn't, Mr. Manning. Say, when you get your gear taken care of, come over and have supper with us. My girl's the best cook on the river."

This was a quick shift, Mark thought, but it was the way men of Engle's caliber performed. Try a bluff and if it doesn't work, get down on your knees quickly before you get hurt. Why not make friends with him? Mark thought. The girl attracted him. Perhaps it was her indifference which was a challenge. Or maybe it was curiosity. In any case she was a capable-looking girl who didn't deserve an incompetent bluffer for a father.

"Glad to, Engle," Mark said. "How soon?"

"Oh, about half an hour," Engle said, and nodded pleasantly and walked away.

Mark filled and lighted his pipe, then went to the river and returned with an armful of driftwood that was dry enough to burn. He would need a fire for breakfast if not tonight. Then he stretched out on the ground, his eyes on the sky that was turning scarlet in the west, and he let his mind turn back to the years that had followed his father's death.

5

George Manning was one of the first half-dozen men to be buried in the new Achilles cemetery located on top of a bare, wind-swept ridge. From that point on a clear day a man could look at the snow peaks of the Continental Divide not far to the west on one side, or for miles across the foothills and the plains on the east.

Mark's father had always liked this spot. Many times he had got out of bed in the chill of dark morning and dressed and come up here to watch the sunrise. In the evenings of days he had missed seeing the sunrise, he had often told Mark to tend the store while he climbed the ridge to watch the sunset.

He never discussed his thoughts during these moments of silent beauty, but Mark suspected that he put his mind on God or on his wife. Perhaps, Mark decided, she had found a way to communicate with his father during these moments when night became day or day became night.

On the day his father was buried Mark listened to the preacher read from the Bible, he heard him pray and heard him preach and heard him eulogize his father, but it was all distant and unreal and a sort of lie. No one, the solemn-faced preacher least of all, understood George Manning.

After the funeral the miners came into the store and talked to Mark, and in their rough way tried to sympathize with him. He sat there, listening politely and wishing they'd go away and leave him alone. Presently they did leave, all but the sheriff of Gilpin County who had come up from Central City.

"I can't leave you here by yourself," the sheriff said fretfully. "I'd give you a home, but I've got six kids and I just ain't got the room."

"I'll be all right," Mark said. "I'm George Manning's son. He raised me to look out for myself from the time I was a little kid."

The sheriff shook his head. "No, I can't leave you here no matter how you was raised." He scratched the back of his neck, then he said, "How much money did your pa have here in the store?"

"A little better'n two hundred dollars."

"Didn't he have money in some bank?"

"No, he didn't trust banks. Anyhow, he wasn't rich. He used what he made in the store to buy more supplies. We got a living out of it. That was all."

"But damn it, he had a good business," the sheriff said.

Mark shrugged. "I can't help it. He'd just brought in a load of merchandise. It's here in the store. Several hundred dollars' worth."

"Well, I'll take the money and put it in a bank in Central City," the sheriff said, "and I'll sell the stuff that's here. Maybe I can find somebody who'll buy the whole kit and kaboodle and I'll put the money in your name along with the cash. Of course there'll be some expenses. The funeral and such."

Mark nodded, thinking there wouldn't be much left for him when it was all wound up. He wouldn't say anything about the money his father had buried under the bed. He didn't know how much was there, but it was more than a thousand dollars. No matter if somebody bought the store, the money would be safer where it was than in the sheriff's hands.

"I'll find a place for you to live," the sheriff said. "Some nice home where you can help out with the work and maybe go to school."

"I never went to school," Mark said. "Not more than a few days here and there anyhow. My father taught me at home. He taught me better than any teacher would. I'm not going to school now."

The sheriff sighed. "All right, Mark. You stay here tonight. You pack your things and I'll come back in the morning and get you soon as I find a place for you to live."

"I told you I'm George Manning's son," Mark said. "He raised me to look out for myself. If I don't like the place you find for me, I'll run away."

The sheriff left, shaking his head and thinking he had never met another boy like Mark Manning.

Mark was lucky. He was given a home by an old German named Franz Sigel who had a tailor shop in Central City. Mrs. Sigel was fat woman who was a good cook and liberally sampled everything she made. Mark worked in the shop, and although he didn't like it, he put up with it, patiently waiting until he was big enough to make his way as a man.

He had been right about what would be left to him of his father's money. The sheriff sold the store and told Mark regretfully that by the time his father's debts were paid and the funeral expenses taken care of, there was less than fifty dollars to be deposited in the bank for him.

Mark looked directly at him and said, "I guess I can't do anything now, but someday when I'm a man I'll come back here and I'll have an accounting."

"You accusing me of cheating you?" the sheriff flared.

"That's just what I'm doing," Mark said. "My father didn't owe a dollar to any man."

The sheriff cursed him and called him an ungrateful pup and would have struck him if Franz Sigel hadn't come into the room. He said, "You'd better go, Sheriff." The sheriff obeyed, muttering under his breath.

When Mark had a day off, he visited Achilles, always going to the cemetery. He would stand beside the grave and look at the mountains on one side and the jumble of hills and canyons and the plains beyond on the other side, and all the time he hoped that his father would find a way to speak to him, but he never did.

After a year the mines petered out and Achilles became a ghost town, most of the buildings empty, but the man who bought the store remained for three years because there was a good deal of traffic between Central City and the other mining camps beyond Achilles. One day when Mark was fifteen he discovered that the store was vacant, the owner having cleaned off the shelves and moved on. He had left the building empty, the loose windows to rattle in the wind, the pack rats the only occupants.

Mark found a shovel and, shutting the front door, began to dig. The money was where George Manning had left it, more gold than Mark had ever seen before in his life. He took it back to Central City and showed it to Franz Sigel, the only man he trusted. He asked the tailor what he should do with it.

Sigel scratched his head and frowned. "I dunno," he said. "I don't like banks. They go bust. If I get a little ahead, I buy property. Houses you rent."

"But houses burn down," Mark said.

"Yah, that is true." Sigel said. "You know anything better?"

"No," Mark said. "I don't."

"Then you buy houses," Sigel said.

He did, with Sigel's help. There was $1020 plus the $50 he had in the bank. Sigel paid him a small wage which was enough to buy his clothes. A year later when he was sixteen he was as big as the average man and strong enough to do a man's work, so he told Sigel he was leaving and asked Sigel to look after his property and to bank the rent after taking out something for his trouble. Sigel agreed to do this, although he was sorry to see Mark go.

The next years were drifting ones, and that was the way he wanted it. He went to Idaho Springs, then up Clear Creek to Georgetown where he found work in a mine, and back downstream to Golden. There he worked in a livery stable, and although he liked horses, he hated his job, so he quit and went on into Denver.

He found that Denver was not much like the settlement on the banks of Cherry Creek where he had lived with his father the first winter they were in Colorado. Too many people now, too much ugliness and filth as his father used to say about the bigger mining camps, so he hooked on with a freight outfit that operated between Denver and South Park.

Still his feet were itchy; there was much to do and see. He bought a horse and rode south to the Purgatory where he got a job on a cattle ranch. He settled down there, liking the work better than any he'd done before. He heard from Franz Sigel now and then. The tailor reported that his bank account was growing slowly, but he should return to Central City and look after his property himself.

When Mark was twenty-two, Sigel died, so Mark decided he'd better go back to Central City. His boyhood years in that area had left two very strong memories in his mind. One was the way the sheriff had cheated him when he was a boy of twelve. He had never forgotten the accounting he had promised the law man.

Mark stood six feet two inches and he weighed one hundred seventy pounds. He was strong and hard-muscled, not the knotty muscles of a blacksmith or a woodchopper, but the long, sinewy muscles of a riding man. He had been taught by necessity to use his fists and he was a good hand with a gun. He would never, he thought, be better fitted for demanding and securing an accounting than now.

The second memory was of the murder of his father. The years had not dimmed the picture that had been burned so deeply into his mind. He hated crime and he hated men who committed crime, and nothing had happened in the eleven years since then to alter that hatred.

He had thought a great deal about his father during these years, and now he saw him in a different light than he had as a boy. Not that he thought the less of him, for his father had given him time and attention and love, and that, he knew, was more than many men gave their sons. But he was able now to recognize a weakness in his father he had not sensed as a boy.

George Manning had been a mild and gentle man who for some reason had been afraid of life. That could have been the reason he had not married again and had actually been afraid of women. He had been thoughtful, he had possessed strong convictions about human problems, yet he had never lifted a hand to solve any of them.

He had hated slavery, but he had not fought to destroy it. Mark knew that his father understood a great deal about God and life and death, and yet all he could do about the meanness and the evil that was in the world was to ask the question: Why do men do the things they do to each other?

When Mark arrived in Central City, he made up his mind. He would do more than ask questions. In a way his life was an extension of his father's. Perhaps George Manning had understood that all the time.

In Central City Mark learned that death had cheated him on one more score. The sheriff who owed him the accounting was dead. The new sheriff was a young and forthright man who needed a deputy. Mark took the job, seeing in it an opportunity to do some of the things his father had only thought about.

6

Mark, his thoughts far from this moment and this camp beside the Gunnison, was jarred from his reveries by Will Engle's strident voice, "Come and get it, Manning, afore we throw it out."

Mark got up, knocked his pipe out against his boot heel, and dropped it into his coat pocket. He crossed to the Engle camp, the smell of the bubbling stew a mouth-watering fragrance in his nostrils.

Engle motioned to the girl who stood beside the fire. "My daughter Laura, Manning. Mark, didn't you say?"

"That's right. Mark Manning." He smiled at the girl who held her hand out to him in a direct, manlike gesture. He said, "You're very kind, inviting me to supper."

"We're glad to have you." She drew her hand back, her gaze touching his face briefly before she turned away. "I don't pretend to be much of a cook out there, Mr. Manning. We have stew when we can, but vegetables and fresh meat are hard to get."

"Meet Charley McGivern, Manning," Engle motioned to the old man who had been in the river tugging at a pile of driftwood when Mark had ridden by. "He works for me. Drives a wagon and he'll help me start my store when and if they ever let us onto the reservation."

Mark shook McGivern's hand. He was in his middle or late sixties. He was skinny to the point of being cadaverous, the yellow skin of his face above his beard pulled tightly over his cheekbones. His fingers and hands were long, almost clawlike, the bones rolling limply together under Mark's grip. He mumbled, "Pleased to meetcha," and withdrew his hand from Mark's.

Mark said, "Howdy, McGivern," and thought that here was a poor excuse of a hired man, but if he had measured Engle correctly, McGivern was the kind he would want to work for him. He would be afraid of anyone younger and stronger who had ideas and a driving will of his own. Not physical fear, Mark thought, but the greater fear of having his cloak of pompous dignity stripped from him before the eyes of his daughter.

Laura had laid out tin cups and plates and knives, forks, and spoons. "Help yourself," she said.

McGivern obeyed with alacrity, his liver-brown lips twitching with anticipation under his skimpy beard. Mark's eyes turned to Laura who was glaring at McGivern. She was a tall girl, five feet six inches or so. She had long legs and a strong big-boned body with none of the pretended fragile qualities which Mark had come to associate with women, but still she was wonderfully feminine. She would stir any man, he thought, although he had a feeling she was not aware of this ability and would not have valued it highly if she had.

Her lips were full, her mouth sweetly shaped. Her eyes, Mark thought, were the brightest blue he had ever seen. When she was younger, her hair had probably been red, but age had darkened it until now it was more auburn than red. She wore a green blouse, a brown riding skirt, and buckskin vest that had been made soft by use and was showing the long wear it had received.

"Mr. Manning, if you've finished inspecting me, will you fill your plate?" Laura said.

"I'm sorry." He was embarrassed by her directness and knew that he was blushing. He added, "I've been on the trail a long time. I just haven't seen a pretty girl lately."

"Now you've paid for your supper," she said testily. "Go ahead and eat it."

In spite of her tone of voice, he thought that she was pleased. He poured coffee into a cup, filled his plate and helped himself to the biscuits, then squatted beside the fire. McGivern had crossed to a log and had sat down and was eating noisily.

Engle dropped down beside Mark. "Ever been here before?" he asked.

"Yes. I worked for the Agency four years ago. I rode past here on my way into the reservation."

Engle looked at him, quick eagerness showing in his face. "Then you're familiar with the reservation."

Mark grinned. "I ought to be. Not all of it, of course, but I've been up and down the Uncompahgre as far as its junction with the Gunnison."

"Then tell me something. What would you say was the best site for a town?" He motioned to the wagons. "I've brought supplies for a store. Whisky, tobacco, guns, ammunition, canned grub, beans, rice. You know, the things these people will have to buy when their stock runs low, but I think the money is in a town site if a man picks the right location."

Mark nodded agreement, knowing that was true, but he had a feeling that Engle was the kind of hardhead who listened to everyone and ended up by doing the opposite to what he had been told. Mark had never met a man who had the exaggerated sense of self-importance that exuded from Will Engle who was worth a damn.

"I'd say there were two spots where someone will start successful towns," Mark said. "One is where Cedar Creek come into the Uncompahgre. It's just about where the road hits the river. Rivers and smaller streams always have determined the routes of transportation and they always will. A railroad is bound to come into this country and it's my judgment it will be built down Cedar Creek. If you miss the railroad, you're dead."

"I see, I see," Engle said. "Now about the other site you mentioned?"

"Where the Uncompahgre and the Gunnison come together," Mark answered, "but it would be my second choice. It's farther downstream and therefore will be slower developing. A third possibility is where the Gunnison and the Grand meet, but that's a long ways from where you'll start the run. Besides, it might be years before it's settled enough to make anyone a profit."

Engle's face had turned grave. "I had in mind a site farther upstream from what you're talking about. Closer to the fort. A man will pick up a lot of business from the soldiers."

Mark nodded and was silent. Engle had made up his mind and was disappointed that Mark had not arrived at the same conclusion he had. When Mark said nothing, Engle asked, "Well, what do you think?"

"I've told you what I think. You ever been on the reservation?"

"No, but I've studied the map. It's the fort I'm interested in. You see, this is my chance, the kind of opportunity that comes to a man once in a lifetime. I ain't going to miss it. I'm going to make my stake while the soldiers are still in the valley. They're big spenders, Manning. Give them a place to drink and buy tobacco and play cards and you can't miss."

"What's the news from the reservation?" Mark asked.

"Nothing," Engle grumbled. "By God, we've tried to find out something. We stop soldiers when they ride past. Captain Cline who has a ranch inside the reservation comes by here on his way to Gunnison once in a while and we ask him, but he claims he don't know. We even sent a man to the fort, but that damned Colonel Mackenzie won't say anything."

"Maybe he doesn't know," Mark said.

"Or care." Engle said harshly. "Last April I read in the newspaper that the commissioners, Otto Mears anyway, said it was risky giving the order for the Injuns to move until they had troops. Well, now they've got troops but nothing happens.

Engle got up and kicked savagely at the fire. "Sometimes I think they've forgotten us. Six, seven hundred people just waiting to get onto the Injun land. Wasting our time here. Scrounging around for wood. Eating up our resources while the summer goes past. And why? I'll tell you, Manning. Just so they can coddle a bunch of damned heathens."

This was the kind of talk Mark expected from Engle, the same talk he would hear from nearly every camper along the river. Although he had known this was the feeling, that for months the cry all over Colorado had been "The Utes must go," it still irritated him to hear it.

"There's the Indian side of it," Mark said. "They're being driven off their tribal home land by force and they're probably thinking of everything they can to slow up their removal. You can't blame them."

"The hell I can't." Engle put down his empty plate and glared at Mark. "I don't care nothing about the Injuns. Ignorant, bloodthirsty boogers. That's all they are. Look what they done to Meeker. And ambushing Thornburgh and killing him. If I was Colonel Mackenzie, I'd move 'em tomorrow or I'd wheel my cannons up and mow 'em down. We got here a month ago. I was afraid we'd be too late, with all the talk about how the Utes were finally going to go, but here we sit just like the day we got here."

He shook his head angrily. "No, I tell you, Manning. I was in the Army during the war. Got wounded at Wilson's Creek and was discharged. I've been out here in Colorado ever since. Almost twenty years. I know, I tell you. Put the right man in command and the soldiers would do the job, but Mackenzie just sits and waits."

"The right man," Mark said softly. "Like Chivington, maybe?"

"That's right. I was in Denver when he ran the redskins down at Sand Creek. He saved our lives. If it hadn't been for him the plains tribes would have got together and wiped Denver off the face of the map, and look what he got for doing his duty."

Mark rose and, walking to where Laura sat, put his plate and cup and silverware on the ground beside her. He knew that if he kept on talking to Engle, he'd wind up hitting the man and that would not solve anything. He wouldn't change Engle's way of thinking if he beat him half to death.

"Will you take a walk with me before it gets plumb dark?" he asked. She looked at him, hesitating, and he added, "It's a pleasant evening."

From the log McGivern slapped at a mosquito and swore. "Biggest mosquitoes I ever seen in my life," he said.

"They sure are," Engle agreed. "You know, Manning, a bunch of 'em lit on a man the other day. Just down the river a piece. Seems like they got their bills into his feller and they stuck there, and then they all started flapping their wings at the same time. Well sir, they just lifted that poor devil off his blanket and carried him away. You know we ain't seen him since.''

Engle slapped his leg and laughed immoderately. McGivern snickered as if knowing it was expected of him. Mark didn't laugh and he didn't turn around to look at Engle. The sun was down and the twilight was fading so he could not see Laura's expression clearly, but he had the feeling that this joke was more than familiar to her.

She murmured, ''Yes, I'll go. It will be chilly soon. I'll get my shawl.''

She disappeared into the tent. Mark walked to the road, wanting only to get away from Engle before he said or did something he would regret. Laura had his sympathy. He thought how little he knew about women, at least the decent kind he wanted for a wife. There had been so few in Central City or on the reservation when he'd worked there. Or any place where he'd lived.

He took his pipe from his pocket and filled and lighted it, his mind crowded again with memories.

7

Mark kept his job as deputy for nearly two years and then resigned. He considered his experience valuable, but he did not find the work as rewarding as he had expected.

He sold his property at a loss, for Central City was past its boom days. Or perhaps property values still reflected the ravages of the financial panic of '73. At any rate, he took the best offer he could get, but when he rode out of town, he carried only $1200 in his money belt. Even with the rental money that had been banked through the years, he had very little more than he had dug up in gold in the back room of his father's old store.

For a time he rode aimlessly, knowing that he wasn't ready to settle down. He thought a good deal about his father and his father's unanswered question. He thought about his two years as deputy, too, but the only conclusion he came to was that jailing, shooting, beating, and hanging criminals did not settle anything. At times these acts were necessary, of course, but they reminded him of sitting on the lid of a kettle of boiling water in the hope the water would be prevented from boiling over.

Nothing was solved. Causes were not analyzed. Nobody gave a damn about what happened to the men who committed crimes. Society had its revenge. The law-abiding citizens said smugly that it served the murderer right when he swung at the end of a rope, that the robber who went to prison got off easy, but at the same time Mark knew that some of the smuggest and most articulate among the law-abiding citizens were criminals themselves in a slightly different sense of the word. Like the crooked sheriff who had cheated Mark out of several hundred dollars when he was a boy, there were far too many who were honest only when it wasn't safe to be crooked and who walked a narrow line between being inside the law and outside.

Butchers bought stolen beef, pretending not to know it was stolen. Horse traders swapped for stolen horses, blandly accepting forged bills of sales as if they believed them to be genuine. There were politicians, bankers, land speculators, mine owners, railroad, and toll road builders—he could add to the list indefinitely—who traded favors while serving as elders of the churches and leaders of their communities, sure of their salvation and of the truth of their concept of God, and never once gave thought to the notion that there was a very thin line between their acts and that of an armed robber. If anyone had made such an accusation, these men would have screamed so loudly in outrage that they would have been heard from one end of the newly formed state of Colorado to the other.

Sooner or later Mark returned to his father's question: Why do men do the things they do to each other? And he added a question of his own. Why did his father who had never injured another man have to die the way he had?

There were no answers, of course, but it didn't do any good for Mark to say to himself that they were foolish questions, that he'd be better off to forget all of them and go out and make as much money as he could in any way that he could. He had too much of George Manning in him to stop asking questions. He would go on asking them as long as he lived whether there were any answers or not.

Before the fall of 1876 was over his restlessness drove him over the Continental Divide to the Ute reservation. He foresaw that a gigantic crime was in the making, although no one was calling it that. Politicians, business men, newspaper editors, common men who sought cheap land: all looked across the mountains to the sprawling reservation that made up most of the western slope of Colorado and were envious. So the cry was taken up: The Utes must go.

No, it wouldn't be called a crime. Perhaps the term was manifest destiny. Some might even be inadvertently admitting the truth by saying that to the mighty who were victorious belongs the spoils. No one except a natural maverick like Mark Manning would ever call it a crime.

Mark took a job at the Los Piños Agency and remained there a year. He helped with the Agency herd, working out of the cow camp which was located at the junction of the Uncompahgre and Cow Creek. He took his turn carrying mail from the Agency to Lake City which meant riding more than seventy-five miles of rough country before he struck the Lake Fork.

In his off hours Mark went hunting in the timber to the south, often bringing in a wild gobbler or a buck. He took part in the debates and plays that the Agency employees put on in a big tent which had been put up to serve as a waiting room for the Utes who had business with the agent.

Most of the Utes spoke broken English and nearly all of them knew Spanish. Mark had picked up enough Spanish when he had been on the Purgatory to talk with the Indians if they couldn't manage English. He found to his surprise that they had a great sense of humor, they were long-winded talkers, and the men were the world's champion loafers.

On occasion when Mark was carrying mail a band of Utes would stop him and demand that he open the letters and read them aloud. They wanted to know what the agent was writing to Washington about them. "Heap big talk," they would say sullenly, and Mark knew that many of their grievances were valid. No agent, regardless of his honesty, could settle them satisfactorily. Mark refused to open the letters and then the Utes would threaten him. All he could do was to warn them he'd tell Ouray. This never failed to cool them off and they let him go on, the letters still unopened.

He became friends with the important chiefs, particularly Ouray and his wife Chipeta, who was the most charming squaw he had ever seen. Ouray was head chief of the Tabeguaches, the band which lived on the Uncompahgre. The government recognized him as chief of the Seven Confederated Bands of Utes, but some of the bands lived in the south along the Colorado-New Mexico line and others lived in the north on White River, and these tribes never officially gave him such a title, although on major affairs he did exert considerable influence upon them.

Ouray believed in peace, partly, Mark supposed, because he had been to Washington and had seen with his own eyes the power and wealth of the whites. Mark often visited him and Chipeta on their farm which was downriver from the Agency. He cultivated sixty acres of land and owned a large band of sheep and goats. His house, which was furnished as well as any white man's in the area, was made of adobe and had several rooms and a shingle roof.

Ouray wore his hair in long braids, but in general he dressed like a white man and tried to show his people that they could learn the white man's way of life. In this he failed, for to most of the braves farming belonged to the women.

Mark knew Sapinero, Ouray's brother-in-law, and liked him. He despised Colorow, a huge man burdened with a load of fat who, with a band of malcontents, had roamed far from the reservation and scared settlers' wives by demanding something to eat. He often talked war, but Mark suspected he was a coward at heart.

Mark's favorite was Shavano, a war chief who, with Ouray, had fought many battles in his youth with the Cheyennes and Arapahoes and Comanches, and, according to the stories Mark heard, had never been defeated.

A young man died shortly before Christmas and was

buried on top of a hill a mile from the Agency. The agent read impressively from the Episcopal Prayer Book, snow falling all through the service, but it was Shavano's part that impressed Mark. Most Utes stood while they prayed, but Shavano had spent some of his early years with Catholic priests at Santa Fe and had been taught to kneel in prayer. This he did beside the grave.

Shavano's prayer was given in Spanish, but Mark translated it as he listened. "May the Great Spirit that lives in the sun have mercy on his soul that he may go to where our forefathers live in the 'Happy Hunting Grounds' and be forever at home. In a little while he will go to the sun and see the Great Father of all the Utes."

He rose then and said, "*Poca tiempo vamoosa por sal.*" He pointed upward with a forefinger, repeating twice in English, "Pretty soon he will go the sun." He joined the circle of whites. Later, when the rites were finished, Shavano and six other Indians rode past the grave, their hands extended in the air. This, Mark understood, was an expression of sorrow for the one who had died.

Mark thought about this a great deal in the time he was on the reservation. He wished his father could have seen it. He would, Mark thought, have felt the same way he did, that these primitive Indians lived closer to God and understood Him better than most whites for all of their dogmas and ritual.

Ouray never said so in words, but Mark had a feeling that the Chief realized the Utes' time in their hunting and fishing paradise was limited. War was no answer, for in the end they would lose, and if they weren't hanged, they would certainly be moved to Indian Territory or possibly to Florida. So he tried to delay the loss of their land as long as he could, sometimes even writing letters to the President in Washington stating his grievances.

Mark had no prophetic vision, but he knew that sooner or later the Utes would lose their land and the white man would move in regardless of all the treaties that had been signed in the past. One year. Three. Five. He couldn't guess, but when the time came, he would return and take his quarter section of land. He had never seen any other valley he liked as well as that of the Uncompahgre.

He rode a great deal. He looked down into the awesome depths of the Black Canyon of the Gunnison to the north. He rode to the top of Grand Mesa, said to be the biggest flat-topped mountain in the world. He visited the Uncompahgre Plateau that from the valley made a long, almost level line against the sky. Finally, before he left, he picked the spot he would take. Not on the river where most people would settle first, but on a mesa to the south where the red loam was rich and deep and not at all like the adobe soil on the other side of the river that would be the hardest kind of land to farm.

He left the reservation at the end of the year, the old restlessness in him again. He would save his money and add to it if he could. He'd buy cattle, for the Uncompahgre Valley was certainly one of the finest cow countries in the world, with summer range on the plateau that would make the stockmen east of the mountains shake their heads with envy.

He was riding for a ranch on the Arkansas below Pueblo when he heard the Meeker Massacre on White River in the fall of 1879. Major Thornburgh, coming to Nathan Meeker's assistance, was killed and his command pinned down for six days. Meeker and all the men at the Agency were murdered. The three women who were there and two small children were kidnaped by the Utes but finally released, largely due to Ouray's influence.

No one had to be the seventh son of a seventh son to know that this was all the excuse the whites needed. The cry, "The Utes must go," grew louder and shriller all over the state of Colorado. Ouray died the following summer, and Mark wondered if his death had been hastened by the growing pressure of a destiny he could not alter.

Still, it was another year before the white man's greed for land finally won the struggle. So Mark, the savings in his money belt now $1450, returned to the Gunnison to wait for the final word, his father's question still unanswered.

8

Mark waited only a few minutes until Laura joined him, a blue shawl over her shoulders. She turned upstream without a word, walking in leggy strides. He fell into step beside her, his admiration for her growing. Neither talked for a time, but it was a companionable silence and not one of cool indifference. He had, he decided, completely mis-judged her when he had first seen her beside her cook fire.

He wondered what she thought of her father and if she had welcomed this opportunity to escape for a short time from his company. It was unfortunate, Mark thought, that people could not choose their parents.

When they reached the camp of the two women Mark had passed that afternoon, he asked, "Is there a man with this outfit?"

Laura glanced at him sharply. "Why do you ask?"

"No reason except that I was curious. When I rode by the young woman smiled as if she'd like to be friendly, but the big one stopped chopping wood long enough to motion me to go on."

"We're all curious," Laura said. "No, there isn't any man with them. The big woman says she can do anything a man can and I believe her."

"What's her name?"

"Effie Allen. The young one is Ann Collins." Laura hesitated, then said, "It isn't any of my business, but if you want to get acquainted with Ann, you had . . ." She stopped, then added, "I'm sorry. I shouldn't have said anything."

"Go ahead. Like I said, I was just curious, maybe because of the way the big woman was chopping wood. She swung the ax like a man."

"She's like a man in a lot of ways," Laura said. "Ann wants to be friendly, but Effie acts like she's jealous. Or something. I don't know what it is. She just makes it plain that she's too busy to visit."

"Folks leave her alone?"

"We have to, and that's hard on them. You know how it is in a crowd of this kind. We have all kinds of people. Good, bad, and indifferent. I guess most of us are the indifferent ones you'd find anywhere. We've got some bad ones, two anyway that everybody's afraid of. Barney Burris and Dave Rawlins. We don't know yet if they're really bad, but they're ornery.

"Rawlins is good-looking and knows it. I guess he liked Ann and tried to talk to her. Effie picked a fight and beat him up. He couldn't get away and he didn't want to hit a woman, and Ann couldn't make Effie stop. I don't know what would have happened if Burris hadn't come by and pulled Effie off."

"That's what you started to warn me about, wasn't it?"

"Yes," Laura said, "then I thought it sounded like I was butting into your business."

"You might have saved me some trouble at that." He paused and then said, "That name you mentioned, Barney Burris, is familiar. What does he look like?"

"Big," she said. "Not tall, but big and mean and strong. He's built like an oak stump. He has the thickest neck and shoulders I ever saw on a man. The ugliest face, too. He likes to fight and he always wins."

"Now I remember," Mark said. "I arrested him once in Central City. He'd been in a fight with an old man and almost killed him."

"You're a law man?"

"Not now. I was a deputy in Gilpin County for a couple of years. I don't remember the other man, though. This Rawlins. They must have hooked up later."

"I don't know about that," she said. "They aren't anything alike. You wonder what they see in each other. It's like Effie and Ann. A queer pair to be together." She paused, and then said, "It's getting pretty dark. Maybe we'd better go back."

They turned, Mark asking, "What about a man named John Draper. I met him on the road and for a minute I thought I had been transported back in time to Old Testament days."

She laughed. "That's just about what I said to Pa when I first saw Big John. That's what everybody calls him. He's a preacher. I guess you found that out."

"I sure did. He doesn't leave any doubt about it."

"Well, there's a lot he wouldn't tell you and you wouldn't know, just looking at him. He's a blacksmith, too. That's the way he made a living before he came here. When he has church, he doesn't take an offering. He says the

Apostle Paul earned his living as a tentmaker and the least he can do is to shoe horses, but this summer he hasn't worked. He says we need a preacher. He doesn't own anything except the pack on his back. He sleeps along the river under a tree. People ask him to eat with them, so I guess he doesn't worry about buying food. He's given away most of the money he had to people who are needy. We have them, too. Women and children, I mean. Some of the men go to Gunnison too often and throw their money away.''

"I guess there are always some like that."

They were silent again for a time, then Laura said, "I hope you won't think I'm prying, but it's my turn to be curious. Most of the men along the river are farmers, but I don't think you are."

He laughed. "No, I'm not a farmer and I don't want to be. I mean, I'm not going to raise hay and beans and corn and such to sell, but I'll take a piece of land and I'll raise what I have to. I'm going to have a cattle ranch. I've got my place picked out and I aim to get there first."

She sighed. "I'm afraid there are times when I wish I was a man. That's what I'd like to have, but Pa's got his head set on having a store. He'll lose all of my money if I let him."

"Your money?" Mark asked before he thought, then added quickly, "I'm the one who's prying now, but if it's your money, you have a right to say how it's spent."

"I didn't intend to say that," she said, angry with herself. "I'm not going to talk about it. It's my problem and I won't burden you with it. I do have some money which I'm keeping. Maybe we could be partners . . . I mean, if you had a place where you could run a few more head than you can buy . . .''

She stopped. "Oh, you'll think I'm as bold as brass and I guess I am. I'm sorry, Mr. Manning. I don't usually talk to men like this that I've known only a few hours. It's just that since I was a little girl I've wanted to have cattle. I don't know why, really, unless it seems to fit this country. Or maybe it's because it's a free life. As free as anyone can have.''

"That's the way I feel," he agreed. "I've had a lot of different jobs, but working with cattle is the only thing I've liked. When you work on another man's ranch, you take his orders and you're a long ways from being free. I guess that's what brought me back to this country. Until it's settled up, and it won't be crowded for a while, a man can make money with cattle. Your idea might be a good one. I don't have all the money in the world. If I get the land I want, I'll be able to take care of a few more cows than I can buy."

"Then we'll wait and see," she said.

They had reached her camp. As she turned toward her tent, he asked, "Will you take a ride with me tomorrow?" She stopped and swung around slowly, but in the darkness he could not see her face. He had no idea what she was thinking, and when she didn't answer for a moment, he wondered if he had made a mistake asking her. He added, "If you've got work to do, I wouldn't want you to . . ."

"I don't have any work that won't keep," she said, loud enough for her father to hear. "I'll be glad to go with you in the morning."

She ran to her tent, ignoring her father who sat beside the fire smoking his pipe. He rose and walked toward Mark. When he reached him, he took his pipe out of his mouth and said slowly, "Manning, Laura's all I've got. I don't want nothing to happen to her."

"You're saying that something might happen to her if she went riding with me?" Mark asked softly.

"Hell, I don't know nothing about you," Engle said. "You just rode in from I don't know where and you camped beside us. I asked you over for a meal, but that don't mean you've got the right to come nosing around . . ."

"That's up to Laura," Mark said. "If she says she doesn't want to see me, I won't bother her, but *she'll* have to tell me, not you. You tried one bluff on me today, Engle. It didn't work. This one won't, either."

Engle backed off, spluttering, "Damn it, I just don't want Laura to get . . ."

"You know something?" Mark asked. "She'll be safer riding with me than sitting here with you."

Mark pushed past Engle, leaving him standing there

staring after him. Any responsible father would act just as Engle had. He would have been remiss if he had not said what he had, but Mark could not let him interfere.

Later, with his head on his saddle and his blankets over him, Mark stared at the sky through the leaves of the cottonwood, the stars brighter and clearer and closer in this high, cold air then he had ever seen them before, and for the first time in his life he told himself he had met a girl he would like to have for a wife.

2

Laura Engle

1

Laura rose before sunup, built a fire, and started breakfast, then she called her father and Charley McGivern from where they slept inside one of the wagons, and returned to the fire. She had slept very little during the night. She had no intimate knowledge of men; she knew very little about love of any kind, at least since her mother had died when she was ten.

The men did not get up, so she went back to the wagon and called them again. She saw that Mark Manning had a fire going. The morning was chilly as nearly all mornings were at this altitude. The sun was up now and the day would be warm unless a thunderstorm rolled down from the mountains, but the night would be cold again.

She wondered what the weather would be like on the reservation. Warmer, she thought, perhaps even hot, and the winter would not be as severe as it was here on the Gunnison. The altitude was much lower. Perhaps it would be similar to the weather at Canon City where she had lived the last three years.

Her father finally crawled out of the wagon and walked

toward the fire yawning and rubbing his eyes. She asked, "Charley?"

"He's getting up, I guess," Engle said, and went on toward the river.

She threw more wood on the fire and held her hands out to the flames. She glanced toward Manning's camp again. He was bending over the frying pan, his back to her. She felt like a school girl with her first crush. Just looking at his back started her heart to pounding. She wondered if he liked her just a little. He must, she decided, or he wouldn't have asked her to go riding with him today.

She'd had only a few dates with boys the last year she'd lived in Canon City. They had been her age, all of them wild, loud, and lacking any sense of responsibility. They'd end up like her father, she thought. No, probably not. Most men matured somewhere along the line. Mark Manning had. She didn't know how old he was. Thirty, maybe. Ten years or so older than she was. Perhaps that was why she liked him. Probably he'd had his day of crazy youth, too, but it was behind him.

He was a man in every sense of the word, and she liked everything about him that she had seen or heard or sensed. That was the difference between him and her father. Will Engle had never matured. He was still a boy as far as responsibility went and he would be a boy when he died.

Her father returned from the river just as Charley McGivern crawled out of the wagon, yawning and belching and scratching the back of his head as he went past them to the river. Her father squatted beside the fire and filled a tin plate with salt side and flapjacks, then poured a cup of black steaming coffee. She filled her plate, too, and poured coffee into her cup.

She wasn't hungry, but she didn't know how much of a ride Manning wanted to take, and she had no time to fix a lunch. She would take a sack of biscuits and a small jar of strawberry jam that she had made before she left Canon City. Not much of a lunch, but it would have to do. Now she had better eat while she could.

"Laura."

It was Mark Manning's voice. She glanced up, surprised

that he had called her by her first name, but pleased that he had. She said, "What is it?"

"How soon will you be ready?"

"About half an hour."

He nodded as if that suited him and returned to his fire. Engle said in a low, bitter tone, "I don't want you to go with him. Tell him you have too much work to do."

She stared at him. She hated him, she told herself. She had every reason to hate him. He never had been the kind of father he should have been. She asked herself as she had so many times why had she given in to him on this store idea. He would fail as he had failed at everything he had ever tried, but this time it was her money he was throwing away.

Well, she should know if anyone did what Will Engle was, and still she had let him talk her into it. Talking was the one thing he did well. She'd held out five hundred dollars. He knew she had some left, but he didn't know how much. She wouldn't tell him, either, and she certainly wouldn't let him have it no matter how persuasive his reasons were.

She wouldn't even tell him where she kept the money. Mere biological chance had made him her father, and that was the only reason she had let him have the money. A poor reason, she told herself bitterly.

"Laura, did you hear me?" Engle asked.

"I heard you," she said. "I think you know I'm not going to pay any attention to your orders. I thought we had that understanding before we left Canon City."

Charley McGivern came to the fire, still yawning and scratching. He said, "Hell of a cold morning for August, ain't it?"

Neither Engle nor Laura paid any attention to him. Engle put his plate down and stared at her, then he said in a complaining tone, "Laura, I don't have any living kin but you. You're flesh of my flesh. I just couldn't stand it if anything happened to you."

She lifted her gaze to meet his. She said, "Pa, you never used to say that when I was little and didn't have any money."

He glanced away, his face turning red. "You shouldn't

say that," he muttered. "I guess I didn't take care of you very good, but I tried. Things never worked out for me. You know that."

"You've got your chance now," she said. "I've given it to you. Whatever I owed you, I've paid back. Not let me alone."

McGivern was eating as noisily as ever. He lifted the coffee cup to his mouth and drank, making a slurping sound. Laura shuddered and put her plate and cup down. If she had to live with McGivern for the next year and listen to him eat and drink, she'd lose her mind.

"You can clean the dishes up this morning," she said.

Engle looked hurt as if this was a great indignity. She started toward her tent, then stopped when her father said "It ain't that I don't like this Manning feller. It's just that we don't know nothing about him. You can't tell what he might do to you when you get a long ways from here."

It was true, but still it startled her. She had the feeling she knew Mark Manning well. She said, "He's a man and I think he's a gentleman. I trust him." She paused, all the old bitterness and anger at her father for his failures and neglect boiled up in her and she said in a low voice, "It's funny how concerned you are about me now that you know I still have a little money left. When I took the job keeping house for Ed Mallory you weren't worried about me. But then I didn't have anything but my wages."

Engle stared at the fire. "You ain't got no right to keep talking that way," he said. "I did worry about you when you were in Canon City. I always have worried."

McGivern belched with satisfaction as he reached for more flapjacks. "Cold enough to freeze the behind off a brass monkey," he said. "Wonder what it's like here in the winter?"

Laura said to her father, "You worried about me the same way you worried about Ma, I guess." She whirled and went into her tent.

In a moment she came out, wearing her flat-brimmed hat and a leather jacket. She carried a sack with the biscuits and the strawberry jam. She saddled her horse that was staked out across the road with the other animals. Her father had said it was a waste of money to buy a saddle horse. She could ride in one of the wagons, but on this one point she had been adamant.

Once they were settled on the reservation and she was keeping house for her father and McGivern, she would be tied down twenty-four hours a day if she didn't have a saddle horse. She had looked around Gunnison for several days before settling on this four-year-old bay gelding she called Fox. She had ridden him every hour she could spare since they had camped here and she had no reason to regret her bargain.

She took longer than usual to tighten the cinch, standing with her back to the camp. She would say yes, she told herself, if Mark Manning asked her to marry him. Crazy to even think of such a thing, but she would. Of course it would be a gamble, but any marriage was a gamble.

The truth was she couldn't go on living with her father and McGivern, and she shrank from going on to Ouray or Silverton or Telluride or any of the mining camps and trying to make her living. She didn't have enough money to start a business, so she'd have to go to work for someone else again. Even if she got a job keeping house for some bachelor or widower, she would never find another man as easy to work for as Ed Mallory.

She sighed and told herself she was a fool. She was old enough to know better. Mark simply wanted someone's company to while away the hours of waiting. She had better look at it the same way.

She had been so busy with the horse and her thoughts that she had not been aware that Dave Rawlins and Barney Burris had ridden up. She had no idea they were anywhere around until she turned and saw them. She froze, holding the reins in her right hand.

Rawlins smiled at her, his hungry eyes on her. He was the most handsome man she had ever seen, perfectly proportioned and graceful of body, with light blue eyes that she was never able to read. He had asked her for dates on several occasions and she had always turned him down. She was afraid of him, although she didn't know why. He had never given her any reason to feel that way. He had always been respectful just as he was now.

He touched the brim of his hat as he said, ''Good

morning, Miss Laura. It seems that I got here just in time
to go riding with you.''

She glanced at Burris who had reined up beside Rawlins, a massive man with big bones and hard muscles. And
cruelty, she thought. She sensed an animal-like brutality
about him that made him a little less than human. Maybe
she imagined it because of the stories she had heard of the
fights he'd had since he had come to the river two weeks
ago, or maybe it was because of his ugliness of face. His
big nose, thick lips, muddy brown eyes, and low forehead
reminded her of a fat, malevolent toad.

''Well, Miss Laura,'' Rawlins said. ''If you're ready,
let's start out. Which way do you want to go?''

''I'm not going with you,'' Laura said. ''I'm going with
Mr. Manning.''

She motioned toward Mark's camp. Rawlins frowned,
glancing at Mark who, having tightened the cinch, had
turned to look at the visitors. Will Engle and Charley
McGivern were silent watchers from their fire, both afraid
that they would somehow be involved.

''Another new one, Barney,'' Rawlins said. ''Coming
in all the time like a plague of locusts.''

Burris leaned forward in his saddle, staring at Mark who
was walking slowly toward him. He said, ''Dave, I've
seen this jasper somewhere.''

Rawlins shrugged, dismissing Burris's words as if they
were of no consequence. ''Your name Manning?''

''That's right,'' Mark said.

Rawlins turned his head to Laura, then back to face
Mark. He said, ''Tell the lady you don't feel like riding
this morning. She's going with me.''

''You're mistaken,'' Mark said. ''I feel very much like
riding and she is going with me.'' He nodded at Burris.
''Well, Barney, from what I hear, you're still making
trouble. I guess we didn't teach you anything at Central
City.''

''By God, that's it,'' Burris said as if he had just seen
the light. ''I'll settle with this bastard, Dave. He bent a
gun barrel over my head in Central City and threw me into
the calaboose. I had a headache for a week.''

''Well now,'' Mark said, ''if you are going to settle

something with me, this is a good time. I never like to see a man put things off.''

He was silently laughing at them, Laura saw, and she began to tremble. No one had stood up to these men since they had come to the river. Everyone, unless it was Big John Draper, was afraid of them, or at least of Burris. But it was plain that Mark wasn't. He was acting as if he would welcome trouble with them.

Now she was seeing a part of him she had not suspected last night. He stood with his right hand close to gun butt, balanced easily on the balls of his feet as he waited for a hostile move from either man. Laura stifled an impulse to cry out to him that she wanted him to live, that this was suicide and there was no reason for it.

"All right, Manning," Rawlins said cheerfully. "I guess it is your turn to ride today. I'll wait for mine. Come on, Barney.''

They spurred their horses into a run, going upstream toward Gunnison. Laura felt weak as if her knees could no longer hold her upright. She heard Mark ask as if nothing had happened, "You ready now?"

She nodded and, turning to her horse, stepped into the saddle. She couldn't say anything. She started riding south through the low sagebrush across the valley that tipped upward from the river and suddenly she began to cry from sheer relief. Mark caught up with her a moment later. Surprised, he asked, "What's the matter?"

She wiped her eyes with the sleeve of her jacket. "Don't you know what you did?" she asked. "You almost got yourself killed.''

He grinned and shook his head. "No, they were the ones who almost got killed and Rawlins knew it. That's why he decided to back down.''

"But they're the men I told you about," she said. "Burris has run roughshod over everyone from the day he got here. Rawlins is usually with him so I don't think he's any better.''

"I guess no one knew how to handle them," he said.

"You were magnificent," she said softly, and looked away, afraid that her feeling for him could be read in her face.

Whatever she did, she must not throw herself at him, must not make her feeling too obvious. That would be a fatal mistake. So for a long time they rode in silence while Laura thought how it had been with her.

A woman had a right to expect some things from marriage. Not always love perhaps, for some marriages were for convenience. A man needed a housekeeper, a woman needed a home, some security, a place of refuge from the hardships, the suffering, the privations of a hard life in a hard country. Or was that too much to ask of marriage? Her mother had had none of them.

2

Laura did not know that her mother was dying, but she was only ten and she had never seen the face of death before. She stayed beside her mother who lay on a pallet in a covered wagon near the mouth of Clear Creek canyon just above the town of Golden. Laura's father had gone to find a doctor, but he had left hours ago and he should have been back long before now.

Laura's mother didn't say anything. She lay on her back, her thin hands folded over her breast, her eyes closed, every rasping breath a struggle. The cold October wind that funneled down the canyon struck at the wagon and slipped in under the canvas. Even though she was covered by several quilts, Mrs. Engle chilled so that at times her teeth chattered and her thin body shook uncontrollably. Laura could not do anything for her. Her mother had not been warm since the weather had turned cold in September.

The sun had dropped down behind the ridges to the west. It would be even colder before long. Laura, huddled beside her mother, shivered and pulled the ragged blanket tighter around her shoulders in an effort to protect herself from the wind, but she lacked warm clothes and the blanket was threadbare. All the good covers, and they weren't very good, were spread over her mother.

Laura had been cold for a long time, too. This had been a chilly fall with very little Indian summer. Laura was hungry, so hungry she wanted to cry, but she had learned

a long time ago that her mother felt worse when she cried.
There had been nothing to eat for weeks but beans, and
they were gone now. Laura and her father had finished
them last night. Her mother had eaten nothing for several
days.

Her mother's eyes opened and her hands made a fluttery
motion. She whispered, "Be a good girl, Laura. Take care
of your father. He needs someone to take care of him."

She shut her eyes, then she whispered, her voice so low
that Laura had to bend over to hear what she said above
the scream of the wind, "Your father volunteered to fight
for the Union in the Civil War, but he was wounded in the
battle of Wilson's Creek. He was discharged and came
home and married me. He did one brave thing, Laura. One
. . . brave . . . thing."

She didn't say another word. A few minutes later she
shuddered, her mouth sagged open, and her hands fell away
from her breast. She didn't move again. Laura said, "Ma."
Then she cried out, "Ma." But there was no answer. She
did not recognize death for quite a while, and when she
did, she could not hold the tears back any more.

Her father finally returned at dusk without a doctor. He
climbed into the wagon, saying loudly, "I couldn't get a
single damned doctor to come. They wanted to know if I
had any money, and when I said I'd have to pay them
later, they said they were busy." He was only then aware
that Laura was crying, and he demanded, "What's the
matter with you?"

She couldn't answer for a while. When she was older,
she wondered if he went for a doctor at all. He had a
senseless kind of pride. Even though he had failed at
everything he had tried to do and never had more than a
few dollars in his pocket at a time, he did have this strange
pride which made him try to hide his poverty behind an
irritating mask of importance.

It was probably, Laura thought in later years, that he did
realize how desperately ill her mother was and he simply
walked the streets of Golden hoping to find a job that
would give him enough money to pay a doctor. Failing at
that, he lacked the courage to go to a doctor and say he
needed him but could not pay for his services.

Her father lighted a lantern and asked again, "What are you bawling for? It won't make you no warmer."

She said then, "I think Ma's dead."

She would never forget his startled expression. Perhaps it had not occurred to him that his wife was mortal and could not go on living year after year hungry and neglected as she had been. Quickly he moved to her, holding the lantern so the murky light fell upon her gray, stony face. He cried out then, and sat down. He set the lantern beside the pallet, slowly and carefully, and bowed his head.

After a long time he put an arm around Laura and hugged her hard. He said, "I swear to you, Laura, that this will never happen to you. Somehow we'll change things. I won't let you grow up hungry all the time and freeze like this. You're going to school. You're going to be a fine lady."

He meant it. She didn't doubt it then and she never doubted it later. But for Will Engle meaning something and actually doing it were two very different things. He did get a job in Denver working for a stage company and he kept it through the winter. He rented a small house and Laura went to school for a full term, the first and last time she ever did. When the good weather came, he was on the move again.

Laura, her child body so thin she looked frail, had to grow up and become a woman overnight. As her mother had said, Will Engle needed someone to take care of him. Laura soon realized what her mother had meant. If she lived to be a hundred she would never understand how any man could have such good intentions and still fail so miserably at everything he tried.

He never held a job very long. It wasn't, Laura decided when she was still very young, that he couldn't do the work or that he was physically lazy. He usually lost his jobs because he tried to tell his boss how to run his business, and no man could stand those words of wisdom coming as they did in the know-it-all tone Will Engle used on such occasions. Sometimes he simply refused to take orders, claiming that he had been insulted. No one, he'd say, who had any pride could be expected to stand such treatment. Not Will Engle.

Never, in Laura's hearing, did he admit that his failures

were his fault. He would lay his trouble on President Grant, on Congress, on the governor of Colorado, on the tariff, on his stubborn, damn-fool boss who didn't recognize intelligent suggestions when he heard them. If he ever remembered the promise he had made to Laura the night her mother died, he failed to mention it.

They traveled as far south as Trinidad, crossed the Sangre de Cristo Range into the San Luis Valley and came north again, using the same covered wagon in which Laura's mother had died. Sometimes they had enough to eat, sometimes they didn't, and when they did, Laura often suspected that the food they were eating had been stolen.

As she grew older, she realized that whatever moral backbone he had once possessed was degenerating, that he would do almost anything for money if it were safe. Of course holding up a stage or train or bank wasn't safe, so he never attempted anything of the kind. Somehow he escaped being arrested, perhaps because petty larceny was the worst crime he committed, and he was shrewd enough to escape detection, or possibly his crimes were so minor they did not warrant prosecution.

Laura started working when she was twelve. The first job she had was in a boardinghouse in Boulder at the west end of Pearl Street. She was still so small that she had to stand on a stool to wash dishes at the sink. Her father was in and out of town all winter visiting one mining camp after another, working a few days and quitting, or following some will-o'-the-wisp rumor of a gold strike. Always, he said, this was the time he would be lucky, but he never was. When spring came, he headed into the mountains for Central City and took Laura with him.

She grew gawky and tall and failed to fill out, but she had an amazing reserve of vitality that enabled her to do any kind of work she attempted. She looked and acted older than she was even at the age of thirteen. Once she succeeded in getting a job, she held it as long as she wanted it or her father would let her. She would never, she promised herself, be the kind of person her father was.

Usually when she found a job that paid her a little money plus her room and board, Engle would let her stay while he took off with his team and wagon. Hope always kept him on the go. He would kiss Laura good-by and tell her, with every indication that he believed it, that this time he would hit it big, that a man's luck was bound to change. She was glad to see him go, and glad to see him come back. Good or bad, he was all the family she had.

She became a good cook, a fastidious housekeeper, and a skilled seamstress. She made her clothes, even her hats, and so had to buy nothing except her shoes and stockings. She learned by hard experience to get the most out of a dollar.

She was willing to try almost any kind of work, but usually she cooked in a restaurant or waited on tables or kept house for some bachelor or widower or a man whose wife was an invalid. All the time she hoped she could find work on a cattle ranch, but she never did.

The summer she was sixteen, her father stopped for the night in Canon City. She was traveling with him, heading toward booming Leadville where she expected to find work, but by sheer accident she found it in Canon City. Her father had left the wagon near the Arkansas River and had staked out the horses while he went to town to look around, as he put it.

As usual, Will Engle had no money, but he would be back before dark and expect Laura to have supper ready. She had a few dollars left from her last job, so it was up to her to buy the groceries.

As she was returning to the wagon from the nearest store, she saw a man ahead of her on crutches. When she came closer, she noticed that he had a wooden leg. He was moving slowly, staying in the dirt along the edge of the street instead of the boardwalk. He was probably afraid, she thought, that he would get his peg leg stuck in a knothole or between the boards.

She glanced at him as she passed. He looked up for a moment and she smiled at him and went on. He was about thirty-five, she guessed, a good-looking man, although his face was extraordinarily pale. She was curious about him and glanced back before she reached the corner. Just at that instant a buggy came careening around the corner, the driver yelling and whipping his horse like a mad man.

Perhaps the driver was drunk. Laura never knew, and

she never knew, either, whether he had aimed to run the crippled man down or not. He didn't, largely because the man with the wooden leg got out of the way, but he moved too fast and lost his balance and fell headlong across the boardwalk. The buggy disappeared on down the street, the driver turning his head and yelling back derisively.

Indignant, Laura hurried to the crippled man. She put her groceries down and helped him sit up. He had twisted his good leg when he had fallen and was in great pain, but he held back the groans.

After a time he said, "About ten feet more and I'd have been off the street and in my own yard. I live right here." He nodded at the white cottage beside him. "If you'll go for help, I'd appreciate it."

"I don't want to leave you," she said. "Let me see if I can help you up."

He protested, but he was not a heavy man and she succeeded in getting him up on his good leg and his crutches under his arms. Every step he took must have been agony for him, but with Laura's help, he struggled through the gate in the picket fence and across the yard and up the steps.

He had to rest then, sweat pouring down his face. She opened the door and held the screen back, and he finally managed to stay upright long enough to reach the leather couch in his front room. There he collapsed. He could not, she thought, have gone another step.

For a time he sat motionless, his eyes closed and his teeth clenched. His pulse hammered in his forehead as sweat ran down his face. She hurried into the kitchen, found a pan and filled it with water and, grabbing up a towel, hurried back. She dipped one end of the towel in water and wiped his face, then dried it.

"Let me take your shoe off," she said. "I think you sprained your ankle when you fell. It's swelling."

He shook his head. "Don't bother about that. I'm sorry to bother you, miss, but I need a doctor. Doc Fisher lives three blocks from here. It's just down the street. Would you go see if he's home? Tell him Ed Mallory had a bad fall."

She nodded and ran out of the house, leaving the grocer-

ies in the street where she had dropped them. She brought
the doctor, and while he was examining Mallory's leg, she
built a fire in the kitchen stove. She brought the groceries
in, forgetting all about her father for the moment.

Before Doc Fisher left, he came into the kitchen and
said that Mallory would have to stay off his good leg for a
week or more. Then he said Mallory had just lost his
housekeeper and the doctor couldn't think of anyone he
could get to come and take care of Mallory on a moment's
notice. Would Laura stay? Mallory would pay her, of
course.

Laura said she would be happy to take care of Mr.
Mallory, not dreaming that she was taking a job which
would last for three years until Ed Mallory died.

3

Laura and Mark Manning nooned beside a small spring
in the aspens on a hillside far to the south of the river.
They ate the biscuits and strawberry jam, drank from the
spring, and lay back in the grass to stare at the cottony
clouds above them that drifted slowly across the cerulean
sky.

Mark filled his pipe and lighted it, then propped himself
up on an elbow. He said, "Funny thing, all those people
back there, waiting to grab the Indian land the minute the
Army says they can and getting madder every day because
they're still having to wait."

She nodded. "I hear about it every day. I guess Pa must
be the worst of the lot. The way he talks you'd think the
Army was determined to keep him off the reservation."

Mark laughed. "You just hear more about it from him
than your neighbors, but I'll bet they're all talking the
same thing." His face turned grave, and he added, "But
you're here and I'm here, and I guess we don't like the
waiting any more than your dad does."

"No, you're different," she said quickly. "I mean,
you're not like the others. Everybody would be a little
different if we knew their history, but we're all alike in
one way. We're greedy, looking for cheap farm land or a
town site or something, but I think it takes more than

greed to make a person leave his home and pioneer a new country like this reservation.''

"Oh, I don't know," he said. "Maybe it depends on what you're leaving. I didn't have a home. I was just riding for a big cattle outfit and I wasn't getting anywhere. You never get anywhere working for somebody else. I guess I'm here because I'm greedy and I want cheap land the same as everybody else.''

She flushed, embarrassed. "I didn't mean it that way. Not the way it sounded." She sat up and folded her long legs under her. "You're a man who could make a success out of anything you set your mind to, but if you could get the truth out of Pa, and I think it's the same with most of the others, they'd tell you they hadn't made a success out of what they were doing, so they're looking for another chance.''

He nodded. "I suppose so, although men like Dave Rawlins and Barney Burris are the same wherever you find them. By hook or crook they manage to live off the labor of someone else.''

"They're different from most," she admitted. "So are Effie Allen and Ann Collins. And Big John Draper." She bit her lower lip, her gaze fixed on his face, then she said, "Mark, what I'm trying to say is, well, take Pa for example. He thinks that once he gets on the reservation it will be a brand-new life, but it won't. He'll carry all of his old faults and his old problems with him.''

"That's right," Mark said. "There's an old saying that a leopard can't change his spots and it's true. Your father and no one else will find the Uncompahgre a paradise, so a lot of them will be gone in a year. By that time the railroad will be there and we'll get a new crop of settlers, maybe this time with some money to invest." He knocked his pipe out against his heel. "Why is your father making this move?''

"Because he's a failure," she said passionately.

"You told me you let him have the money to start a store," he said.

"Yes, I loaned him the money," she said bitterly, "and that makes me just as foolish as my mother. I knew it, too, but I went ahead and did it just the same. He told me he never had a chance. All he needed was a start in a new country, then he'd make it. Well, he is my father. I can always go to work again somewhere if I have to, so I gave him the chance he says he's never had. Now it's up to him.''

Mark filled his pipe, saying nothing, but she sensed the question that was in his mind, so she told him how she got the job with Ed Mallory.

"He was a good man," she aid. "Goodness is something you can't define, but you can feel it in another person. I felt it every day in Ed. Maybe it was the suffering that made him that way. You see, he lost a leg in the battle of Glorieta Pass. That's why he studied law. He was a good lawyer. At least he had all the business he could handle. He wasn't very strong and he didn't like to go to court because it was hard for him to get around. He had rheumatism and his stump hurt him. I guess he was in pain all the time.

"I took care of him the best I could. I used to rub his back and his leg, and at night when he couldn't sleep, I'd get up and build a fire and heat some bricks and wrap them and lay them beside his leg and back, then he could sleep until morning. He'd had other housekeepers, he said, but none of them took care of him the way I did.

"I was a skinny girl when I started working for him. After I'd been there about a year he said I had filled out. Most of the time I hadn't had enough to eat and hadn't even had a good bed to sleep on. I'd worked too hard, I guess. For my age, anyhow. After I went to live in his house he gave me plenty of money for groceries. I had my own room and a good bed. If I was up at night with Ed, I could always sleep the next day."

She stopped, staring northward across the hills toward the Gunnison, but not seeing them, not seeing anything except the mental pictures of those good days with Ed Mallory.

"You filled out pretty well," Mark said, smiling. "You're an uncommonly pretty girl, Laura."

She glanced at him and looked away, blushing. "Thank you." She paused, and then hurried on. "I often wonder what would have happened to me if I hadn't been there when he fell and I'd kept on the way I was, working a while and then moving on with Pa in his wagon. He was always after something that wasn't there. Well, after he gets tired of the store, he'll sell it or give it away and start out again."

She moistened her lips with the tip of her tongue. "Ed told me that's what Pa would do. I mean, he warned me Pa would never settle down and make a success of anything. He didn't like Pa much. You see, when I went to work for Ed, Pa just moved in. Took his meals at Ed's table. Left his wagon in Ed's back yard. Put his team in Ed's barn. That didn't last long. Ed told him he would visit me for three days at a time. No more. Pa pulled out in a huff, but he came back after a while, stayed his three days, and left again. That's the way it went all the time I was there.

"Ed said he was a parasite and maybe that's what he is. Anyhow, after I'd worked for Ed for about two and a half years, he told me he was leaving everything he had to me if I'd go on taking care of him till he died. He said if I got married, my husband could stay there with me. At the time I thought Ed would live a long time, but maybe he knew better. Anyhow, he died last spring. He owned his house and a business building downtown and there was some money in the bank.

"Right away Pa started in on me to sell the property and come over here and wait for the reservation to open up. I did finally. I didn't want to live in Canon City anyway. I kept five hundred dollars out. Pa doesn't know how much I have or he'd think of something to buy with it. Well, I don't have any faith in him, the way he's always lived, but maybe he never did have the right opportunity. I decided to see that he had it just once. If he fails now, he can never say it again."

She stopped and shook her head at Mark. "I don't know why I'm telling you all of this. Once I got started, I just couldn't stop."

She knew, though, why she had said as much as she had. She had to be honest with Mark. It was better, she thought, that he know about her and her father now than later, know exactly what their past had been and what the future might be.

She told herself so often that she would never do anything else for her father, never give him another dollar, but
all the time in the back of her mind was the depressing
knowledge that she would weaken when he needed her,
that he would be a burden to her as long as he lived. Or
perhaps as long as she lived.

He had said at breakfast that she was his only living kin.
It was true. Right or wrong, bad or good, biological
accident or not, the fact remained that he was her father.
Nothing but death could change it.

"I think I know why you couldn't stop," Mark said
gently. "You needed to talk to someone. You haven't had
anyone since Ed Mallory died, have you?"

"No one," she said. "Thank you for listening."

"It was good for me to listen," he told her. "I guess we
all have doubts about ourselves and the wisdom of the
things we do. Sometimes we find ourselves doing things
we don't want to. For days you've been wondering if you
were crazy to loan your father the money, haven't you?"

"That's right," she said. "Every time I hear him talking to Charley McGivern or anyone else who comes by as if
he had all the wisdom of the ages stored in his mind, I ask
myself that question."

"I'll answer it for you," he said. "You weren't crazy at
all. You've got to look at it the other way. Suppose you
hadn't loaned him the money? How would you feel years
from now if he told you he had missed his one big chance
because you kept him from taking it?"

"I know, I know," she said. "I have thought of that."

He got up and, reaching for her hands, pulled her to her
feet. "We'd better start back," he said. "We're going to
get wet before we reach the river the way those thunder-
heads are piling up."

For just a moment he held her hands, his eyes probing
hers, and she thought he was going to kiss her. She had
never been kissed, not really kissed by a man she wanted
to love and wanted to love her. There had been plenty of
men who had more than kissing on their minds and had
waited for her in halls and dark corners in the boarding-
houses where she had worked.

She hated them and what they wanted from her; she

kicked and scratched and hit them, and they had been glad
to let her go. But now, for the first time in her life she
stood holding hands with a man she wanted to kiss her,
wanted to be taken into his arms and held so hard that his
embrace hurt her.

He dropped her hands and turned away, saying, "I'll
tighten the chinches. We'd better be lighting a shuck out
of here."

She stood motionless, her hands clenched at her sides,
and fought back the tears. Why hadn't he kissed her? Was
he married? Or in love with another girl? There was no
way of finding out unless she asked him, and she couldn't
do that.

The storm struck before they reached the river, the rain
sweeping across the valley like a visible screen. Then it
was upon them, coming down in huge drops that pounded
at them and soaked them in a matter of seconds, and
rushed on across the sage-covered hills to the south. The
sun came out again and took the wet chill out of the air
and raised a steam from the soaked earth.

When they reached camp, Mark said, "I'll pull off the
saddles. You hit for your tent and change your clothes."
He dismounted and gave her a hand, asking, "Tomorrow?"

She nodded, smiling. "Tomorrow unless you're afraid
you'll get tired of my company."

"That's one thing I'd never be afraid of," he said.

"All right then," she said. "Tomorrow."

She gave him a quick smile and ran across the muddy
road toward her tent. Her father was standing beside one
of the wagons. When she reached him, he said, "Laura,
you've got to tell Manning you won't see him any more."

"I'll never tell him that."

She saw then that he was frightened. He gripped her
shoulders. "Laura, you listen to me. Dave Rawlins and
Barney Burris came by about an hour ago. They threatened
me. They said I'd better see to it that you and Manning
stayed away from each other."

She saw the bleak terror in his eyes, the quiver at the
corners of his mouth, and she realized that this was the
first time to her knowledge that he had ever been completely demoralized by fear. Cowardice was not one of his

failings. Still, it was his problem. She would not give
Mark up because of any threats Dave Rawlins and Barney
Burris had made. They could be faced down. Mark had
done it this morning.

"Pa," she said, "I've taken care of myself since Ma
died. I've even taken care of you when it should have been
the other way around. You'll have to tell Rawlins that I'm
grown and I make my own decisions."

She jerked free from his grip and hurried on into the
tent, her wet clothes clinging to her.

3

Ann Collins

1

Ann Collins felt as if she were a prisoner, which indeed
she was. She never forgot for a moment how much she
owed Effie Allen, or what would happen if she left her.
Still, there were times when she felt she hated her.

This was Saturday night. Later, after it was dark, someone on up the river would build a big fire and maybe as
many as a hundred people would gather around it. Most of
them would be men, she thought, and some would certainly be young and single. Probably one of them would
show up with a fiddle and there would be dancing. But
Effie wouldn't go and she wouldn't let Ann go. It was
hard to tell what she'd do if Ann just walked off without
her permission and went to the dance. Ann sighed, knowing she wasn't brave enough to try.

Effie had the best of intentions and she was honest in all
the things she said and felt. But honesty and good intentions weren't enough. Ann could not go on living the rest
of her life the way she had for the last five years, but she
hadn't reached the point of overt rebellion yet. She wasn't
sure she ever would.

She was a shy girl who lacked both money and confidence in herself. Even at twenty-two she still showed girlish immaturity in her dark blue eyes and her elfin face and the hesitant tone of her voice. She always deferred to Effie. She was compliant and Effie was dominant, and that, she thought with shame, was the reason she was the prisoner she was.

If Effie would just be a little more friendly to others, or even let Ann be friendly. Most people who were camped along the river tried to be friendly. Ann remembered the tall man who had ridden by on a buckskin gelding leading a pack horse in the middle of the week. He had looked at her with interest and touched the brim of his hat to her and she had smiled at him, but Effie had motioned for him to go on.

He had camped just beyond the Engle wagons. Since then he had gone riding with Laura Engle every day and all Ann had to do to know that Laura was a happy girl was to look at her. Laura was tall and long-legged and auburn-haired, one of the most striking-looking women Ann had ever seen, so it was natural for the stranger to be drawn to her.

Ann had no illusions about herself. She was small, with blue eyes and blond hair, and she guessed she was kind of mousy-looking. Maybe the tall man would not have paid any attention to her regardless of what Effie had done. Still, he had looked at her, and he might have returned just to talk if Effie hadn't motioned him on. And then there was Dave Rawlins . . .

Ann had come near to open rebellion because of what Effie had done to Dave. He was the most handsome man Ann had ever seen. He had stopped to visit several times when Effie was gone from camp for a few minutes. He had charming manners. Ann knew very little about men except what she had read in novels, and when she thought about it, she decided that gallant was the word which best described Dave. He would have asked her to go riding with him, she thought. Or go to the dance. Or something.

But Effie had ruined everything. She had come back too soon. She had cursed him and then attacked him, and for a while Ann had thought she was going to kill him. She was big enough and strong enough to do it. More than that, she was perfectly capable of killing a man, particularly one who seemed to like Ann. Now it was fixed fine and proper. Dave would never talk to Ann again. He'd be too afraid of Effie.

Effie came through the willows from the river, striding briskly along as she always did, her head up, her shoulders back. She wore pants, a man's blue shirt, and a battered hat pulled down over her dark brown hair. She carried her fishing pole in her right hand. Her broad face was tanned as bronze as a cowboy's, darker than any other woman Ann had ever seen, but then Ann doubted that there was any other woman in the world like Effie.

"Damned trout sure ain't biting tonight," Effie said in disgust. "I fished hard, too. I wanted to fetch you a panful for breakfast, but I got only one bite and I lost him." She leaned her fish pole against the side of the wagon. "Supper ready, honey?"

"It's ready," Ann said.

"Good. I'm hungry enough to eat raw bear meat." She paused, her dark eyes on Ann's grave face. She asked, "You unhappy, honey?"

"No," Ann said, and then smiled. "Yes, I guess I am, Effie. There'll be dancing tonight and I think we ought to go. We can't live apart from other people all of our lives."

"I figure we can," Effie said shortly.

Effie picked up a tin plate and went to the fire. The meal was practically the same supper Ann had cooked every night since they had left Effie's farm on the Arkansas the last of June: biscuits baked in the Dutch oven, the coals on top leaving a thin sprinkling of ashes over the biscuits, salt side fried perfectly to a crisp, and gravy that Ann made by stirring flour into the grease from the salt side.

Sometimes Ann cooked beans, but it was a slow process at this altitude and tonight she hadn't bothered. She had opened a can of peaches for dessert, an unusual treat because peaches were expensive and Effie objected to everything which was expensive. She had a right to. All the money they had was hers.

When they finished eating, Ann washed the dishes and Effie watered the horses. Dusk was settling down upon the valley, the last of the sunset fading above the western mountains, when Effie returned to the fire. She rubbed her hands together, making a rustling sound, then squatted by the flames and held her hands over them.

"Colder'n a well digger's butt tonight," she said. "I sure would hate to spend a winter up here. If the Army don't move them damned Injuns, that's just what we'll do."

Ann didn't say anything. She had gone to the wagon for her sweater, but now she sat close to the fire, shivering because the sweater wasn't heavy enough to keep the chill out. She knew she should say something. Effie was watching her, sensing the discontent that was in her tonight. Most of the time Effie was the best-natured woman in the world even after working outside all day, but the one thing that upset her beside having a man under foot was what she called Ann's "unhappy spells."

"Well, we won't have to wait much longer for the Army to make 'em move," Effie said. "The newspapers and the politicians have been hollering too long. There's too many of us waiting here, too. They're gonna have to do something."

Ann looked up and smiled and dropped her gaze again. She said, "Let's go to church in the morning. John Draper would like to have us come."

"Reckon he would." Effie cleared her throat. "Something's biting you tonight, honey. That's as plain to see as rat turds in sugar."

"I guess so," Ann said. "I just get so tired of living this way I can't stand it. Not seeing anybody and not talking to anybody but each other, and people all around us."

Effie sighed. "Honey, ain't I took care of you good right from the first day you came to live with me?"

"Yes, you sure have," Ann said. "I'm not complaining, Effie. I know I'm beholden to you."

"Oh, hell, I don't mean that." Effie stood up and rubbed her hands briskly along her pants legs. "I've been happy, having you and looking out for you."

Ann tried desperately to think of something to say that would change the conversation. She knew what was coming next. It always came sooner or later when they started talking this way. But she didn't think of anything soon enough.

"I told you at first I could take care of you," Effie

cried, her voice louder than she intended for it to be. "Well, ain't I kept my promise?"

"Yes," Ann said in a low tone. "Everything except giving me a baby."

"That again," Effie said in disgust. "You want a man to give you a baby, and then go off and leave you the way your pa did your ma? Hell's bells, why does any woman want to suffer just to have a baby? It's fun for the man, but it sure ain't for the woman." She shook her big head. "You're luckier'n you know, young woman."

"I guess I am," Ann said, and hated herself for lying to Effie. "I'm cold. Let's go to bed."

When they lay on the mattress in the back of the wagon, the heavy blankets over them, Ann wondered how long she could stand it. She did not sleep for a long time that night. She lay staring into the blackness while the sound of fiddle music and singing came to her faintly from up the river. She knew why Effie hated men, hated them with a venom that was unnatural and unbelievable in a woman who was as good-natured as she was about most things.

It went back to her childhood and a stepfather who had been a brute, more animal than man. He whipped her time after time. Once, when her mother had been gone for the evening, he tried to get into bed with her. She had been big and strong, even though she was only fifteen. She got away from him and hit him with a stove poker and almost killed him. She ran away from home and never saw her mother again. She didn't want to, she'd told Ann. Her mother had been weak and a fool for living with a man like that as long as she had.

"Maybe she's still living with him for all I know," Effie had said. "She would be if they're both alive. There just ain't any sense in women putting up with men the way they do."

To Effie all men were the same as her stepfather had been. So strongly was this conviction fixed in her mind that she would never change. Ann had long ago realized there was no use to try. But Ann knew that Effie was wrong. Some men like Dave Rawlins were good.

She even considered slipping out of the wagon and trying to find Dave. He was different. He liked her. She loved him. She was sure she did. If she only had a chance to prove it to him. But he would never come back to the wagon and face Effie again, and Ann wasn't sure what Effie would do if he did. Or if she found them together. She might kill him.

It was all foolish thinking anyway, she told herself hopelessly. She didn't know where Dave was and she wasn't really sure he would welcome her. If he didn't and she left Effie, how would she live? No, she couldn't risk it. She had been in that position once. As long as she lived, she would never forget that hot afternoon in the Pueblo hotel room the first time she met Effie.

2

With the temperature well over one hundred degrees in her hotel room, Ann Collins sat beside the open window with the hot wind striking at her. She trembled, wondering if she had enough courage to kill herself. She had two suitcases filled with clothes and thirty cents. That was everything in the world she owned.

Three dimes! Three thin dimes that she took out of her coin purse and stared at them and put them back into the purse and then did it all over again. But no amount of staring at them made them multiply.

She was seventeen, a slender, thin-cheeked girl who looked younger than she was. Perhaps that was the reason she'd had no luck getting a job. She'd walked the streets of Pueblo for days. She had no training; she'd never worked a day in her life for anyone but her mother. She could sew, she could cook, and she could keep house. These were things she had done for years in the small Kansas town where she had lived with her mother as long as she could remember, but it was not the kind of experience that helped her get work.

Ann's mother had been a teacher, so Ann had taken over the care of the house when she was a small girl and had done very well. She never had time for boys. When school was out at four, she went home and started supper. She cleaned house and washed and ironed, and got up early in the mornings and cooked breakfast. She was bright enough to bring home the best of grades and still do very little studying at night.

Ann had no memory of her father. Her mother never mentioned him. Once when Ann asked about him, her mother said he'd been offered a job in the town of Trinidad, Colorado. He'd gone there, but she'd never heard of him since. She guessed the Indians had killed him. His name was Edwin Collins and he had been a carpenter.

That was all her mother would ever say about him. Perhaps it was all she knew. Ann thought about it a great deal. She had no close friends, no one to talk to except her mother, and it was plain that her mother didn't care anything about Edwin Collins one way or the other.

If there were other relatives, her mother never mentioned them. She did say once she had come from a town in southern Ohio and that her maiden name was Smith. Beyond that she would say nothing about her background. As Ann grew older, she began to wonder if her mother was lying about even these simple facts. If she had a family, she had cut herself off from it as completely as she had from her husband.

As long as she could remember, Ann's life had revolved around her mother, so when she died last June from typhoid fever, Ann's world stopped revolving. There simply wasn't anything for it to revolve around. The house in which they had lived for years was rented. The furniture was worth almost nothing. After the funeral, Ann found that her mother's bank account was much less than she had supposed it was.

For a time Ann was in a state of shock. Even at her age she was completely unprepared to make her own way. There was no work in the town where she lived. She might have secured a teaching job in the country, but she couldn't face the unpleasantness of boarding around with the different families. Worse than that was the certainty that she would have some big boys who would make life miserable for her. No, she couldn't do it. She wouldn't last a week.

People were kind enough. The minister, the principal of the school where her mother taught, the neighbors: all took an interest in her and showered advice upon her, but none of them had any answers for her. The truth was her mother had not raised her to make decisions. Now that she was alone, she had no idea what to do.

Her father who had been only a name now became her one hope. A slim one, but she could think of nothing else. Panicky, she took the money that was left after her mother's funeral, and without saying anything to the people who were concerned about her, packed her two suitcases with her best clothes and went to Trinidad. There she met complete failure. No one had ever heard of Edwin Collins, but the worst of it was that apparently there wasn't even any Trinidad at the time her father was supposed to have gone there.

She went to Pueblo because it was a bigger town and she might find work. She tried. She honestly tried, she told herself now as she sat holding the three dimes. She would have done anything, even to getting down on her knees and scrubbing floors, but she couldn't get any kind of a job. What was worse, apparently no one cared about her or what happened to her.

For the hundredth time she put the dimes back into her coin purse and then threw it onto the bureau. She got up and walked around the room. She hadn't eaten all day. She couldn't pay her hotel bill. They'd put her in jail, she guessed. No, they wouldn't. She'd kill herself before she'd let that happen. Then, suddenly, she gave way. There was no hope for her, nothing she could do, no one to turn to. She dropped across the bed and began to cry.

Once the tears started, she could not stop them. She had no idea of time, no knowledge of the sound she was making. She did not hear the door open and close; she did not know that anyone had come in until she felt a hand on her shoulder and heard a sympathetic voice say, "What's the matter, honey?"

"Go away," she whispered. "Let me alone."

She felt the side of the bed dip under the weight of the person who had spoken to her. The voice said, "Now, now, honey. Me going away ain't going to help you none. Did some man get you into trouble?"

Ann stopped crying and turned on her side. She wiped her eyes and looked and wiped her eyes again. A woman sat on the edge of the bed, a big, strong-looking woman

whose broad face was tanned as dark as a man's. She wore
a brown suit and a black blouse. Her hair was pulled back
tightly from her forehead and pinned in a bun. She wore
no jewelry of any kind, no perfume, no embellishments
whatever to help her looks or call attention to her feminin-
ity, but she did show honest concern.

"No," Ann said. "Why should a man get me into
trouble?"

"Because all the trouble in the world is caused by
men," the woman said. "That's the one mistake the Lord
made when He started creating things. He shouldn't have
made the first man."

"A man didn't have anything to do with it," Ann said.
"My mother died."

"Oh." The woman studied her a moment. "Well now,
honey, there ain't much you can do about death. Crying
don't help worth a damn."

"It's not that. I don't have any money. I can't get a job.
I . . . I just don't know what to do."

"I see," the woman said with irritating cheerfulness.
"You go over there now and wash your face and you'll
feel better. Then you come back and tell me about it."

Ann obeyed, the woman rattling on. "My name's Effie
Allen. I've got a ranch down the river a piece. I do all my
own work. I don't need a man for nothing. Fact is, I don't
have a bull or a stud horse on the place. The nearest I've
got is a rooster and come Thanksgiving he'll go into the
pot." When Ann returned to the bed, Effie asked, "What's
your name, honey?"

"Ann Collins."

"All right, Ann, you sit down beside me and tell me
how you got yourself into this fix."

So Ann told her, and when she mentioned that her father
had left home and never come back, Effie broke in. "That's
just like a man. He gets the fun and she gets the labor.
That's the way the world wags. Go on, honey, and tell me
the rest of it. I guess you didn't find your pa, did you?"

"No," Ann said, and finished her story.

"Well, honey, I've been thinking while you've been
talking I sure ain't much on housework. You can come
and live with me if you think you can stand it. A hell of a

lonesome life and we don't have many neighbors, but I like it. I guess we'd be company for each other. Anyhow, you'd have a place to sleep, a roof over your head, and enough to eat. I'll look after you if you want to give it a try. There's just one thing you've got to know. I won't stand for a man being on the place."

"I don't have enough money to pay my hotel bill," Ann whispered. "Of course I'd like to live with you. All I'd ask for is a chance to work for my room and board."

"Then you've got it." Effie rose and smiled as if it were all settled. "Now you just latch up your suitcases and I'll go fetch mine. I've got the room next to yours. That's how I happened to hear you bawling." She walked to the door and then looked back. "Don't you worry about your hotel bill. I'll pay it and we'll go get my buggy out of the livery stable and we'll git for home."

For a moment Ann stood motionless staring at the door through which Effie Allen had gone. In spite of herself the tears started again. Only a moment before she could see nothing ahead except jail. Or suicide. She wiped her eyes with her damp handkerchief, not fully realizing until that moment that she certainly would have killed herself if Effie Allen hadn't heard her crying. There had been no reasonable alternative.

They reached Effie's house before dark. The barn and outbuildings were neat, the stock well cared for, but the interior of the house was a mess. It wasn't much of a house, really, just one big room that was kitchen and front room, and a lean-to barely big enough to hold a bed and bureau.

In the five years that Ann lived there, she never learned to share Effie's hatred for men. She felt a growing compulsion to have a husband and a home, and most of all she wanted children, but it was a need she seldom mentioned to Effie.

She lived through the days and the weeks and the months, all the time hoping that something would happen to free her. Perhaps one of the neighbor boys would think enough of her to want to marry her. Finally one of them did, at least he kept finding excuses to come to Effie's house in the evening, and always when Effie was gone. At least

Ann thought she was gone, but Effie wasn't fooled. She slammed into the house one evening and told the boy to stir the dust getting out of there. When he was gone, she whirled on Ann.

"Ann," Effie said, "if you let another man come around on the sly to see you, I'll kill him."

A week later she sold out and started for the Gunnison Valley, there to wait for the opening of the Ute reservation. Ann went with her. It seemed to her she had no choice.

3

Ann was up before the sun on Sunday morning just as if it were an ordinary-week day. She built a fire and put the coffeepot on, then huddled over the flames, shivering in the early morning chill. Effie was out on the river fishing. She had never been on a good trout stream before in her life. When they were settled on the reservation, she'd be too busy to fish, but now she had both time and opportunity, so it had become almost a mania with her. She had offered to fix a pole and line for Ann, but Ann didn't have the slightest interest in it.

When the coffee was done, Ann poured a cup and sat by the fire. She sipped the coffee, the same discontent in her that she had felt the night before. She owed so much to Effie, yet she hated her, too. She felt boxed in and she could think of no way to escape.

"Good morning, Miss Ann," a man said.

She jumped up and turned, spilling some of the coffee. Big John Draper, the preacher, was walking toward her from the road. He said apologetically, "I'm sorry I startled you, Miss Ann."

She smiled wanly, her heart still thumping. For one crazy instant she had hoped it was Dave Rawlins. "Oh, it's all right, Mr. Draper. I was just sitting here drinking coffee and . . . and kind of daydreaming."

He slipped the pack from his back, laid his staff down and knelt by the fire, his hands held over the flames. "It's a frosty morning for August," he said. "Where's Miss Effie?"

"Fishing. She spends a lot of time fishing."

Draper smiled. "It's a good activity for woman or man. You'll remember that our Lord chose several fishermen to be His disciples." He sniffed audibly. "That coffee smells good, Miss Ann."

'Oh, I'm sorry, Mr. Draper. Would you like to have a cup?"

"I'd be very happy to accept one." He sighed. "I'm a sort of beggar, Miss Ann. I felt that the people camped here needed to hear the word preached and to be ministered unto, and that's the reason I came. I'm busy all the time, yet I sleep under a tree and I have to depend upon the people to feed me."

"Will you have breakfast with us?" Ann asked.

"It would be a privilege," Draper said.

"I'll mix up some flapjack dough," Ann said.

She wondered what Effie would say. Draper had stopped a number of times to visit, but neither Ann nor Effie had ever asked him to eat with them before. The fire of rebellion began burning in Ann as she thought about it. Effie did the hard work and Effie owned the wagon and horses and Effie had all the money, but surely, Ann thought, she had the right to ask a minister to eat with them.

If she didn't, she had better break off with Effie now. Today! She wasn't a slave. Then she took a long breath and shook her head. She might just as well be a slave. She had a right to talk to Dave Rawlins, too, but Effie had denied her that right and almost killed Dave in the process.

Draper's gaze followed every move she made. She was aware of it, and suddenly a great hunger to talk to him almost started the words pouring out of her. But Effie wouldn't like it. Besides, what could Draper tell her? What could he do? Nothing, of course, for her problems were hers to solve. No one, not even a minister, could do or say anything that would help.

She spooned grease into the frying pan and started cooking. She flipped the flapjack and set out tin plates and silverware. Then she saw Effie coming through the willows, a string of trout in her hand.

Effie scowled when she saw Draper. He nodded at her

and said pleasantly, "Good morning, Miss Effie. I see the Lord blessed your efforts this morning."

"I done it all myself," Effie said. "The Lord didn't have nothing to do with it." She handed the trout to Ann. "I cleaned 'em and figured I'd get back before you started breakfast."

"It's not too late. I'll fry them." She hesitated, glancing at Draper who now appeared as fatherly as ever. She said, "I asked Reverend Draper to have breakfast with us."

"If there is plenty, Miss Effie," Draper said. "I don't want to cause either of you extra trouble or make one of you go hungry."

"We've got plenty," Effie said gruffly. "Beside, we've been getting a good chunk of our living out of the river."

"The Lord provides in one way or another," Draper said as if he meant it, and Ann thought that he did.

She handed him a plate with the flapjack on it and spooned more grease into the frying pan, then dropped the trout in. Two of them were so long that their tails extended over the rim of the pan. She poured a cup of coffee for Effie and handed it to her, then she was aware that Draper was standing, an arm raised above his head.

"We thank Thee for this food," Draper prayed. "Bless it so it will strengthen our bodies that we may be able to carry out Thy will at all times. Strengthen our minds against every form of evil and show us the path Thou wouldst have us take. This we ask in Jesus's name. Amen."

He sat down and started to eat. Ann was vaguely relieved. He was indeed a spiritual man. His mind would never descend to sins of the body. She thought happily that maybe she would be saved during services this morning.

When they finished eating, Draper rose and carefully wiped his beard and mustache. He said, "Thank you, ladies, for a delicious repast. It will sustain me through this day of harvest that lies ahead."

"You're welcome, Reverend Draper," Ann said. "I hope you'll stop by again."

"I surely will." Draper turned to Effie who was scowling at him. "Miss Effie, do you know where you will settle on the reservation?"

She was surprised at the question and a little startled,

Ann saw. She hid her smile. She had seldom seen Effie jolted by anything.

"No, I don't," she said. "I've never been there. Have you?"

Draper swung his pack to his shoulders, then stooped and picked up his staff. "No, but I was talking to Mark Manning. He's the man who rode in a few days ago and is camped just below the Engle wagon. I had a visit with him last night. He was kind enough to ask me to have supper with him. He told me he worked on the reservation for about a year, so of course he is familiar with it and the kind of land to be found there."

"Well?" Effie said belligerently.

"It is just a suggestion," Draper said, "but the thought occurred to me that you might like to have a talk with him about it." Again he hesitated, then went on, "This isn't any of my business, but I was wondering if you were going to look for good farming land? Or do you plan to raise cattle?"

"Cattle," she said, "but I ain't sure it makes much difference. I'll tell you one thing, though. I ain't like most of these fools. We don't know when a railroad's coming. Until it does, there won't be no market for corn and wheat and such."

"Except the mining camps," Draper said.

"The mining camps buy beef, too," she snapped, "and cattle can walk to 'em."

"Very well thought out, Miss Effie," Draper said approvingly. "Now it seems to me that Mr. Manning has the same idea. He tells me that the land along the Uncompahgre is spotted. Some is bad, some very good, so it occurred to me that his advice might be valuable to you."

"Thanks," Effie said, "but it ain't likely he's gonna give away any secrets."

He glanced at Ann, smiling benignly. "Perhaps Miss Ann could worm it out of him. They say the way to a man's heart is through his stomach, but a good meal might unlock his lips, too." He turned to walk away, then said over his shoulder, "I hope I will see you at religious services this morning. Perhaps you would like to bring a picnic basket. Most of the families are doing that."

"I'm coming," Ann said, her voice higher and sharper than usual.

"I guess I'll be there," Effie said, "but we ain't bringing no picnic basket." She waited until Draper was in the road, then she said in a low tone, "So you had to ask him to stay for breakfast."

"Yes, that's exactly what I did." Ann stood very straight, her chin thrust out at Effie. She had never defied the big woman in the five years they had been together, but she had to now or she would never be able to have a thought of her own. "You fixed it so Dave won't stop here again. I suppose you won't let me ask Mr. Manning to come for a meal, either. Not even if it meant getting a good piece of land."

"You're damned right you won't ask him," Effie said angrily. "I never needed a man's advice in my life and I don't now."

"All right then," Ann said, raising her voice. "You buy the food I eat and I sleep in your wagon and it's your blankets that keep me warm, but does that mean I don't have any rights at all? Are you telling me I can't even ask a preacher to have breakfast with us?"

Effie blinked. She would not have been more surprised if Ann had struck here. "Oh, honey, don't get mad at me. It was all right. I'm sorry I said anything." Then she took a long breath. "But don't make the mistake of thinking that just because Draper's a preacher he ain't a man. I saw him looking at you. I know what was in his mind. They're all alike. Every mother's son of 'em. They figure a woman is good for just one thing."

Ann turned toward the wagon. She'd heard this talk from Effie for five years and she was sick of it. Effie cried, "What are you going to do?"

"I'm going to get my pink dress out of the trunk," Ann said, "and if you're going to church with me, you put a dress on, too."

"What's got into you?" Effie demanded.

"I'm tired," Ann said miserably. "Tired of being bossed. Tired of you doing my thinking for me. Tired of being told I can do this and I can't do that. For once I'd like to look pretty."

She climbed in the wagon, leaving Effie staring at her,

her mouth open in sheer astonishment. Ann laughed silently as she opened the trunk and took out the pink dress. She had been afraid too long. She should have talked back to Effie a long time ago.

She sighed when she looked at the dress. It was badly wrinkled, but it would have to do. She'd try to fix her hair up a little. Maybe she'd be lucky enough to see Dave Rawlins.

4

Dave Rawlins

1

Dave Rawlins was a lucky man and he knew it. He lay quietly under his blankets while Barney Burris built a fire. He pretended to be asleep, although it didn't make any difference. Barney would start the fire whether he thought Dave was asleep or not. He would take care of the horses and cook breakfast and clean up the dishes, and all Dave had to do in return was to be friendly and compliment Barney now and then at the right times.

When the fire was going, Barney picked up an ax and chopped a day's supply of wood from a drift log at the edge of the river in about the time it would have taken Dave to cut an armload. Dave smiled as he watched Barney swing the ax. He had never seen a stronger man in his life.

But Barney possessed co-ordination, too. It was a pleasure to watch the rhythm of his ax swings and to see the chips fly until the ground was white. Barney demonstrated this same wonderful combination of strength and co-ordination whether he was fighting, swimming, breaking a rough bronc, or doing anything else that required physical effort.

Another interesting quality that Barney had was his sense of loyalty. He carried it to the point of being stupid

about it, a fault for which Dave was thankful. If he wasn't
a little slow in the head, he wouldn't have let Dave take
advantage of him the way he did, but Dave was careful
never to let Barney know that he held him in contempt.
Flattery was the best kind of medicine for Barney and
Dave used it liberally and wisely.

When he finished chopping wood, Barney crossed the
road and led the two saddle horses to the river and watered
them, then he took them back and watered the pack animals. Dave didn't stir until Barney returned to the fire and
started the coffee. He had left his home in Oregon when he
was eighteen, and in the seven years since then he had
thrown in with a number of men, but with none for more
than a few months until he met Barney. The partnership
had lasted for more than a year.

Dave was not a rough man, but he had a cold kind of
courage that had brought him through some scraps that
would have left the average man dead. He was handy with
a revolver, he was a skilled poker player, and he had the
looks and personality that appealed to most men and nearly
all women. He measured and used his own assets almost as
skillfully as he did Barney's with the result that the partnership was as nearly ideal as any human arrangement
could be.

Now, while Barney was busy with the camp chores,
Dave lay quietly watching while he worked on a number
of ideas. If—and this was his careful judgment of himself
—he had a fault which might prove fatal, it was too much
pride. So, knowing this, he watched it closely. Still, whenever he thought of Laura Engle and the cold shoulder she
had given him, he felt as if he were caught in a wild and
turbulent stream and was utterly helpless.

Dave had seldom had any trouble with women, even the
married ones for whom he felt an attraction. Once he'd
had them, he was done with them, but Laura was in a class
all by herself. She had excited him the first time he'd seen
her. He had always been a sucker for auburn hair and tall,
long-legged women. Maybe that was it, along with the
proud way she held her shoulders and her firm breasts. He
had never felt this way about any woman before, and the
remarkable part of it was that he still felt the same attrac-

tion even though she had done everything she could to show him she wasn't interested. To make it worse, she was attracted to this new man, Mark Manning.

When Dave thought of Effie Allen, he was angry because of the beating she had given him. That was all. Just angry. He could and would settle with her in good time. Ann Collins would be his weapon. One look had turned her to soft clay in his hands, but there was no hurry about taking his revenge on Effie.

But there was hurry about his feeling for Laura. She raised his temperature to a fever pitch he could not ignore. It was more than a challenge, yet his common sense warned him that this was something he had to work out. Getting rid of Mark Manning wouldn't solve the problem. Laura had given him the glacial treatment before Manning showed up. No other woman had ever done that, and therefore he had more than hurt pride. He was confused, befuddled, and in danger of losing his self-confidence.

By the time Barney started breakfast, Dave had decided on an idea that would give him some satisfaction even if it didn't do any good. Will Engle was still the only weakness in Laura's armor that Dave could see. So far he had failed with Will. At least his effort to intimidate the man had not succeeded, but he'd continue to work on it because he could find no other pressure point.

"Come and get it," Barney called.

Dave tossed his blanket aside and pulled on his boots and yawned. He went through the willows to the river and washed, and when he returned, Barney motioned to the frying pan and said, "Dig in." After Dave began to eat, Barney added, "This is getting too damned monotonous. Sitting here and waiting and nothing happens. You sashay off to Gunnison and get into a poker game, but I ain't no good at it. I'm gonna have my own kind of fun."

"Like what?"

"Well, I keep thinking about that damned Manning and how he pistol-whipped me in Central City. I think I'll look him up and give him some of what he gave me."

Dave's first thought was that this was a good idea. He sipped his coffee, considering it, and soon realized it wouldn't do. Not unless they could catch Manning by

himself. If Laura saw it, Dave would never have a chance
with her.

"This is Sunday," Dave said by way of gaining time.
"I think we can figure out something better'n that. I'm
sure in favor of having fun, but let's get him some other
day. You know how a lot of these Christers think about
Sunday."

"What do we care about what they think?" Barney
demanded.

"I care about what Laura Engle thinks and you know it."

"You're slipping, Dave boy," Barney said. "I never
seen a woman treat you that way before."

"Give me time," Dave said, hiding his irritation. "I
had a notion of my own about having fun. Laura's dad has
some whisky in one of his wagons. He mentioned it one
time. Maybe we can fix it so he won't get rich off his store
when he gets on the reservation. Whisky is the one thing
he's got that's bound to sell. Why don't we take it out of his
wagon and sell it ourselves?"

"Hell, they'd have the sheriff out of Gunnison right
away," Barney objected.

"Not if Engle didn't know it was gone," Dave sat back
and rolled a cigarette. "Draper's preaching today like he
always does on Sunday. Engle and Laura and probably
Manning will go. They always leave old man McGivern to
look after the wagons. He'll co-operate with us and not tell
Engle, either. I figure Engle won't even know it's gone till
he gets on the reservation and starts looking for it."

"What'll we do with it?" Barney demanded. "Set up a
saloon on the river?"

"Why not?"

" 'Cause somebody will want to know where we got it.
We don't have no wagons. Besides, it might make Engle
suspicious."

Dave had thought of this but he nodded as if it were a
new idea and he admired Barney for thinking of it. He
said, "That's right. Well, there is another thing you can
do. Take it onto the reservation and sell it to Colorow. The
Utes don't have much money, but you can get a hell of a
load of buckskin and that's the same as cash in Gunnison."

"You're loco," Barney said. "You think the soldiers would let me peddle any whisky on the reservation?"

"They'll let you if they don't catch you, and you're too smart to be caught. Wait till night to cross the reservation line and stick to the timber much as you can. You know the reservation and you know Colorow. He'll do business with you."

"The soldiers would hang me if they caught me," Barney grumbled.

"I tell you they won't catch you," Dave assured him. "You're slicker'n a greased pig on the Fourth of July when it comes to a deal like this. You'll be in and out before they know anything about it." He leveled a finger at Barney. "And right now the way the Indians are feeling, they'll do anything to get something to drink."

The flattery did the job as it always did. Barney said, "Yeah, I guess I can do it, all right. You think McGivern will keep his mouth shut?"

"Sure he will," Dave said. "All I've got to do is to show him the point of my knife. Maybe let him feel it on his throat and he'll keep his mouth shut the rest of his life."

"I reckon he will," Barney agreed. "Looking at him is enough to scare him."

"Well then," Dave said as he rose and tossed his cigarette stub into the fire, "I'll shave while you clean the camp up. You'll need to be down the river a piece by the time Draper quits preaching."

Barney had brought a bucket of water from the stream. Dave poured some into a pan and set it on the fire. He wasn't sure whether this piddling robbery was worthwhile or not. The only merchandise that Engle had which was sure to sell was whisky, and from what Engle had said, every cent he had was invested in the goods in his two wagons.

If Engle was broke come fall or early winter, he'd be glad to accept a loan from Dave Rawlins or anyone else he could get it from, but if it came from Dave, there would be a price. He might, he thought with a smile, even be prevailed upon to marry Laura.

His smile widened as he walked to his pack to get his shaving gear. It had been a long time since he'd left Oregon; he had traveled a lot of miles in that time. Women

were made to be taken and left. They'd double-cross a
man if he didn't beat them to it. That was the last lesson
he'd learned just before he'd left home, and the bitterest.

2

Dave Rawlins was born on a farm in the Willamette
Valley near Salem. He was an only child and came late in
the lives of his parents. It was natural for them to consider
it a small miracle, and equally natural that they would
spoil him. He was a cuddly baby, and when he was older
he was a lovable boy, partly because of his curly blond
hair and bright blue eyes and perfection of features, and
partly because his nature was one that demanded affection.

He was, as his mother put it, "the apple of her eye." To
the neighbor women he was "that nice Rawlins boy." If
the church needed an angel for a Christmas or Easter
program, Dave was selected. He was a great favorite of
the girls and was much in demand for parties. On his part,
he was tolerant of girls and accepted his popularity as if it
were his due.

He was not in any way a sissy. There was always much
work to be done on the farm and his father demanded work
from him, gradually increasing his demands as Dave grew
up. The neighbor boys were jealous of him and made snide
remarks about him being pretty. This invariably led to a
fight when he heard the remark, and although he was
slender, he was strong and quick, and there wasn't a boy
in the community his size or age who could whip him.

When he was seventeen, his mother died. His father,
unable to live with his memories, sold the farm and moved
south where he bought some river-bottom land along the
Willamette River near Albany. Within the month Dave
saw a neighbor girl named Ruthie Bales and for the first
time fell in love.

Ruthie was the prettiest girl in the community, a year
younger than Dave but still mature at sixteen. She had
honey-colored hair and hazel eyes and a demure manner
that proclaimed complete innocence. She had her choice of
any of the neighbor boys but competition never bothered
Dave. Time, persistence, charm, and three fights cleared

the field. After that everyone knew Ruthie was Dave Rawlins's girl.

He could have married her any time in the year after that, but he wasn't ready for marriage and never thought seriously about it. He was a little slower developing than most boys his age and it never occurred to him that Ruthie wasn't entirely satisfied to hold hands or have his arm around her in the buggy or share an occasional kiss in the moonlight.

The truth was that the aura of wide-eyed innocence which always enveloped Ruthie was a complete lie. She wanted a man and she had a boy. Since this was something Dave did not even suspect, tragedy was inevitable.

The end came during a Fourth of July picnic on the river. Ruthie went early in the morning with her parents because Dave had to help his father until noon. Ruthie told him she would see that there was plenty of food in the picnic basket and for him to get there as soon as he could. A patriotic program had been planned for the morning and there would be games and races in the afternoon.

Dave's father was a lonely old man after his wife's death and never went anywhere he didn't have to. Dave finished his work sooner than he expected and his father said he could go, so he dressed and hitched the mare to the buggy. He arrived at the picnic grounds a full hour before noon and at least an hour sooner than Ruthie expected him.

He couldn't find her in the crowd, and no one that he asked seemed to know where she had gone, although some of the girls tried to stall him. One of them, a girl who was a year older than Ruthie and who made no secret of her fondness for Dave, asked him to go walking with her. She said that Ruthie had gone off with some other boy or she'd be there waiting for Dave. It was unthinkable and he almost slapped her for saying it.

When he turned and walked away, she called after him, "All right, smarty pants. If you find her, you'll see."

Suspicion began gnawing at him then and he started up the river, his heart pounding so hard it was difficult for him to breathe. He found her in less than ten minutes, although it would have been easy to have walked right past her because she was with a man on the bank of the river behind a thick screen of brush. He would have missed them if he hadn't heard her giggle.

He eased through the brush and stopped dead still. What he saw made him sick. Ruthie was lying on the grass facing the man. She was giggling and playfully pushing him away and plainly not meaning it. The man said, "When are you going to tell the Rawlins kid? I'm going to if you don't."

"I've been going to tell him but, but . . ."

She saw Dave then. The expression on her face told the man someone was there. He jerked his arms out from around her and jumped up. He saw who it was and said, "Oh, it's you, kid."

He worked for one of the neighbors, a transient who didn't have anything and wasn't fit to look at Ruthie, let alone touch her. He heard Ruthie's frightened voice, "Now don't get mad, Dave. I was going to be back in time to meet you."

"Get out of here, kid," the man said contemptuously. "She's my girl now. Can't you see you're . . ."

For one of the few times in his life Dave lost his temper so completely he didn't think of the consequences of his act. He stopped the man's sentence with a punch to his mouth that split a lip and brought a rush of blood. The man was taller than Dave and fifty pounds heavier and stronger, but he never had a chance to use his strength.

He threw a roundhouse blow that missed. Compared to Dave he was miserably slow. Dave smashed his nose, ducked a looping fist that didn't even come close, and then, moving in fast, caught the man squarely on the point of the chin. He reeled back toward the river, stumbled in an effort to regain his footing and went over the edge into a deep hole.

"He'll drown," Ruthie screamed. "You killed him."

Dave whirled to face her. She was anything but demure and innocent now. He said, "I hope he does," and strode through the brush and returned to the picnic grounds. He didn't look back. Ruthie was a good swimmer and she'd probably pull the man out. Dave hooked up and left.

By the time he got home, his anger had cooled off until

he could think coherently. He told his father what had happened, and said, "If he did drown, they'll be after me. If he didn't, I don't want to stay here anyway. I don't ever want to see Ruthie again."

The old man sighed as if he had known all the time that Dave would not stay here. He said, "All right, you take your horse and the saddle and pull out. I don't know where you're going, so I can't tell 'em. I'll give you all the money I've got. After it's gone, you'll have to get a job, but I reckon you'll make out."

He did. He drifted south into California and then into Arizona. He found that he could always get a job. He was that kind of a man. He discovered, too, that he was something special to women. On more than one occasion he had to escape a wrathful father or an outraged husband.

He tried to forget Ruthie but he never fully succeeded. Unconsciously he put all women in her class, thinking of them as cheats and liars, and although he was not fully aware of what he was doing, he took revenge on Ruthie by making love to every woman he could. He never knew how many homes he broke up or how many lives he ruined, and he didn't care. Actually he didn't care about much of anything.

He discovered he could make a living gambling, so he seldom worked. He bought the best of clothes, he always rode a good horse, and he became fast and accurate with the revolver he carried. He never settled down in any place very long. Now and then he threw in for a short time with some other man he took a liking to and then left him when the notion struck him.

He reached Colorado in the summer of 1880. He had never heard whether the man drowned in the Willamette or not. He didn't even hear from his father or know whether he was still alive. Occasionally his conscience hurt him and he considered writing to his father, but his conscience had become too elastic to drive him to any act that was difficult and it was difficult to sit down and write to his father, so he never did.

He ran into Barney Burris quite by accident in a saloon in Del Norte shortly after he reached Colorado. Barney had got himself worked into a corner by three brothers, all

of them taller than Barney and as heavy. Barney loved to
fight, but this time he had tackled more than he could
handle.

Still, he might have whipped the three of them if one
who had been knocked flat on his back hadn't pulled his
gun. Dave seldom bought into another man's trouble, but
this kind of thing outraged him. He pulled his gun and shot
the man before he could pull the trigger. The man didn't
die and the marshal didn't hold Dave. A few days later he
rode out of town with Barney Burris and they just kept
riding together.

Sometimes Dave laughed in silent amusement when he
thought about it, knowing they were a strange pair, but
obviously Barney never gave it a thought. Barney seldom
thought about anything except the next meal or drink or
fight. He worshiped Dave and waited on him and would
have given him anything he owned if Dave had asked for
it, but that was something Dave never did. It was enough
just to have Barney around, for it gave him much the same
satisfaction he would have had if he were being followed
by a faithful dog.

When Dave heard about the reservation being opened in
the summer of 1881 and about the town of Gunnison which
was breaking out at the seams, he told Barney they'd better
ride over the mountains and have a look. There ought, he
said, to be some pretty good pickings in a situation like
that. He was right, but he never told Barney just how good
the pickings were. He had decided months ago that there
were some things it was just as well Barney didn't know.
Money, for instance, and women, Ruthie in particular.

3

Lieutenant Jason Mills of the Fourth Cavalry crossed the
Lake Fork of the Gunnison with his detail shortly after
noon on August 28. When he reached the main river he
sent Sergent Maloney and two men to the north side of the
stream to inform any campers he found that they could
move in the morning. Mills continued eastward with the
remainder of the detail, stopping briefly at each camp to
give the same information to the settlers.

Dave Rawlins and Barney Burris had just finished din-
ner when they herd shouting upstream. "Injuns must be
coming," Burris grunted.

Dave had started to roll a cigarette. He finished, cocking
his head to listen. He heard some hurrahs, and one man
yell, "It's time the Army got off its butt." He said, "It's
not Indians," and, getting to his feet, stepped into the road
so he could see past the point of willows that was just
downriver from their camp. He saw Lieutenant Mills and
his men, Mills talking to the people beyond the willows.

He returned to the fire. "It's the Army. That smart aleck
shavetail we've seen go by here a time or two."

Barney's face turned as pale as it could under the tan. "I
told you that was a fool stunt, swapping the whisky for . . ."

"Oh, for God's sake," Dave said in disgust. "They're
not after us. Colorow and his bucks wouldn't tell and
nobody here knows but McGivern. If he was going to talk,
he'd have done it before now."

"Well, what are they here for?"

"How the hell do I know? Maybe they're finally letting
us move in. Just remember one thing. They don't know
anything if you don't tell them anything."

The soldiers appeared around the willows, Lieutenant
Mills giving the signal to stop when he saw Dave and
Barney. "No wagons?" he asked.

"No wagons and no women," Dave said. "Are we
moving in?"

"That's right," the lieutenant said. "Colonel Mackenzie suggests that the wagons start in the morning, but you
can stay here two or three days if you prefer. You'll move
faster than the wagons. It will be a while before the
Indians are gone and the settlers are allowed on the reservation. Colonel Mackenzie's orders are to stay on the road
and continue past the Agency and the post. Anyone caught
exploring the reservation before the run will be arrested
and thrown into the guardhouse."

"If we're caught," Dave said, smiling.

"You'll be caught," the lieutenant said. "We're patrol-
ling the reservation now and we'll increase the patrols until
the Indians are gone. Any questions?"

"How far do we go?" Dave asked. "To Ouray?"

Lieutenant Mills shook his head. "Hardly. We have drawn a line just above the Agency. You will remain on that line until you are given permission to cross it. The Utes are in an ugly mood and have done their damnedest to delay being moved. We intend to prevent any incident that might lead to bloodshed."

"You won't have any trouble with us." Dave said. "All we want is a piece of land, not a fight."

"I guess nobody wants a fight," Lieutenant Mills said, "but some of the whites don't have sense enough to know they may get one whether they want it or not. We've picked up several settlers already and I suppose we'll pick up more." He paused, his gaze turning to Barney and returning to Dave. "Some son of a bitch sneaked in and sold whisky to Colorow, that's about all it will take to raise hell when moving day comes. You boys have any idea who did it?"

"I sure don't," Barney said quickly.

Too quickly, Dave saw as the lieutenant's gaze whipped back to Barney. Dave said casually, "It's like looking for a needle in a haystack, Lieutenant. Any man on the river might have done it. Or even somebody from Ouray."

"That's right," the lieutenant agreed, "but I'm looking anyhow. If I hear in Gunnison about anyone who traded some buckskin lately, I'll know the man I'm after. The Utes don't have money, but they have ponies and buckskin, and we'd know if a pony herd had come off the reservation the last few days."

Lieutenant Mills nodded and rode on up the river to the next camp. Barney said, "Dave, this is the first mistake I ever knowed you to make, but it's a whopper. That trader Vance won't have enough guts to keep his mouth shut."

Dave grinned. "It was a profitable mistake and don't you forget it. I figure Vance will keep his mouth shut, all right. I told him there'd be another batch if we didn't get caught. He'll wait a long time for it, but he's the kind who'll keep looking."

Barney shook his head glumly. "I've always done what you told me, figuring you were the smart one, but this time I sure wish I hadn't."

"I tell you we'll be all right if you don't get boogery,"

Dave said sharply. "I know what I'm doing. There'll be a thousand people on that line. Even if Vance blabs, which I don't think he will, the Army will have a hard time finding us." He reached for tobacco and paper, turning the problem over in his mind, then he said, "You'd better pack up. The lieutenant won't be back this way till morning, but just to be on the safe side, we'd better be gone when he rides by."

"Now you're talking sense," Barney agreed. "I'd just as soon keep right on going."

Dave shook his head. "Not yet. Too much cream left to skim."

He rolled another cigarette, thinking of Laura Engle. He wanted her as he had never wanted another woman in his life. His feeling for Ruthie had been nothing in comparison to this, but Laura had become cooler and more distant every day, if that was possible. The experience was a new one for him. The pleasure of the game had always been in the pursuit, but this time he wasn't so sure. Possession might even be sweeter. Perhaps Laura was the kind of girl who could make him change his way of life.

"You told the lieutenant we wanted land," Barney said. "You mean it?"

"Hell no," Dave said, wondering uneasily if Barney had read his mind. Only the solid, hard-working kind of man would appeal to Laura, the Mark Manning type. Dave would not, he could not, be such a man, but he could take land, perhaps Manning's. He added, grinning, "If we change our minds and see a claim we like, we'll jump it."

Barney grinned back. "Sure. It'd be easier'n outrunning that bunch."

Barney crossed the road to get the pack horses. Dave kicked the fire out, his temper turning ugly. After all these years how could one long-legged, auburn-haired girl turn him inside out? He didn't know, but one thing was sure: He'd have her if he could, and if he couldn't, Mark Manning would be sorry he ever saw her.

Part 2

The Run

5

Mark Manning

1

Mark left the Gunnison before sunup, arriving at the line above the Agency that evening. It had been a long ride across the Lake Fork, up the twisting switchbacks to the top of Blue Mesa, across the Cimarron and over Cerro to the Uncompahgre. The last leg of the journey past the Army post and the Agency was along the river and therefor easy traveling, but the rest was over a rough country of steep grades and broken mesa tops.

While he was making the ride, Mark kept asking himself how many wagons would turn back, how many would go over the edge of the road that in many places was barely wide enough for a wagon, how many drivers who were unaccustomed to mountain grades would panic and, failing to get the most out of their horses, stall and hold up the entire line of settlers. Most of all, Mark thought about Will Engle and wondered if he should have stayed behind and helped him.

He knew at once the answer was no, for Engle would have resented an offer to help, refusing to admit that he, Will Engle, would have to face a situation in which he needed help. But he would, Mark knew, for the dream world in which the man lived was far different from the world of harsh reality of which the road to the reservation was a part. Perhaps he would not even arrive in time to take part in the run. Still, Mark was convinced that there was nothing he could do, that no one could do anything for Engle until necessity forced him to seek help.

Lieutenant Jason Mills and his detail were on hand to show the settlers where to camp until the word to move onto the reservation was given. He remembered Mark, having spent several minutes talking to him the day before. Several families were already established along the river, so the choice camp sites were taken before Mark arrived.

"These people came down from Ouray." The lieutenant motioned upstream toward the mining camp. "You're the first from the Gunnison except for two fellows named Dave Rawlins and Barney Burris. You know them?"

"Yeah, I know them," Mark said.

"They look like trouble makers to me." Lieutenant Mills said. "Burris anyway. They went on to Ouray. If they want to get drunk and raise hell up there, it's all right with me, but I'm not standing for anything here. I'd guess it'll take the wagons three days to get here from the Gunnison. When they do, they'll be packed in so tight nobody can wiggle. A couple of hard cases like Rawlins and Burris could make a lot of trouble."

Mark nodded, thinking that what the lieutenant said was true, but he didn't want to say anything about Burris's background. Keeping order was the Army's business, not his.

"Camp anywhere you can find a spot," Lieutenant Mills said. "If you want to be out in front when the run starts, you'll have to camp on the bench, but if you like the shade along the river, you'll have to get behind these folks."

"I like shade," Mark said. "I don't suppose I could hold a space big enough for two wagons?"

The lieutenant shook his head. "First here, first served. That's Colonel Mackenzie's orders," he said and rode off.

Mark sat his saddle, deeply troubled as he thought about Laura Engle. Even if her father got here in time to take part in the run, he would very likely be one of the last to arrive and so would have to take whatever camping site was left, probably in the sagebrush near the base of the mesa hill to the west.

This was familiar country to Mark, for he had spent a good deal of time at the Agency when he had worked on the reservation. The camp area was directly upstream from the Agency just below where the hills curved toward the river like giant jaws snapping shut, leaving little more than room for the road to Ouray to follow the bank of the Uncompahgre.

To the west the mesa hill rose in what was almost a sheer cliff. It was on this mesa above the Agency in a forest of piñons and cedars where the young Indian was buried and Mark had been so impressed by Shavano's part in the funeral. Now there were still a few Ute lodges between the Agency and the mesa, but Mark guessed that most of the Indians were already on their way to the new reservation in Utah.

To the east steep adobe hills lifted from the valley floor, their barren slopes slashed by countless centuries of erosion so that Mark used to think he was seeing the deeply lined face of Father Time whenever he looked at them. Above the hill other ridges covered by a pygmy forest rose tier on tier until they were finally dwarfed by a great mountain known as Storm King. It was a fitting name, Mark thought, for he remembered how many times he had seen black clouds swirl around the bulging crest of the peak, then rush down the slope to drench the valley and stab it with thrusts of lightning before the storm moved past to hide the snowcapped peaks of the San Juans.

He rode on up the valley, nodding to the settlers who were camped there. When he was above them, he stepped down, off-saddled, watered both horses, then staked them out in the lush grass along the bank. The long twilight was fading rapidly now, so he hurriedly gathered driftwood and built a fire and cooked supper.

As he was finishing, Lieutenant Mills rode up and dismounted. He accepted a cup of coffee and squatted beside the fire, saying moodily, "It'll be quiet tonight and maybe tomorrow, and then the wagons will be here and we'll have hell in a bucket."

"I didn't hear of much trouble when they were on the Gunnison," Mark said.

The lieutenant shrugged. "It'll be different now. A lot of them have been waiting a long time. When they get here, they'll be so close to what they're after that they can almost reach out and touch it. Even after they get on the reservation, there'll be some bastards who'll try to jump somebody else's claim."

Mark nodded, knowing that was exactly what would happen. There would be fist fights and shootings and maybe killings, and the chances were that in the end the greedy settlers would make more trouble for the Army than the Indians had. He filled his pipe and lighted it with a twig, covertly studying the lieutenant and wondering about him.

Jason Mills was twenty-five or -six, Mark judged, a tall, slender man with thin lips and a sharp nose. He was probably a West Pointer with four or five years of active duty behind him, more than likely in Texas or New Mexico or Arizona. His face was burned by sun and wind until it was nearly as dark as a coffee bean. Indian campaigning had a way of making or breaking young lieutenants just out of the Military Academy, and Mills was a man who would not be easily broken. Still, Mark sensed a brooding discontent in him and he wondered about it.

Mills finished his coffee and set the tin cup down. He asked, trying to be casual, "You know anything about the two women who were camped just above where you were? A big one and a young one named, let's see, Ann Collins, I think."

Mark nodded. "That's her name. The big one's Effie Allen. She's not friendly to anybody, but Ann is. Nobody seemed to know much about them except that Effie runs all the men off who like Ann's looks, so I guess Ann's going to be an old maid. They say Effie likes to brag about being as capable as a man, and after I watched her swing an ax, I believe she is."

"It'd be a shame for a pretty girl like that to be an old maid," the lieutenant said.

"You married?"

"No. Army life's hell on women. They have to move around with their men from one post to another, freezing for a winter in Montana or Dakota and roasting the next summer in Arizona or New Mexico. It's hell these days in the Army, too. I've seen gray-headed lieutenants and captains who would have been generals twenty years ago during the war. Some of them were as a matter of fact.

"They don't make enough to save anything. The other day I heard a wife say that after twenty years in the Army they had a handful of silverware and a pile of cracked plates to show for their life savings. She spent the winter here when they were building the post and damned near froze to death in their tent. She would have if her husband hadn't stayed up most of the nights keeping their Sibley stove red hot.''

Mark nodded, saying nothing. He instinctively liked Mills and didn't want to argue with him, yet he had the thought that if the lieutenant didn't like Army life, he didn't have to stay with it.

''Another thing,'' Mills went on. ''The settlers cuss the Army for not moving the Indians sooner than we have, but they forget what happened to Major Thornburgh and some of his men when they tried to bail Meeker out of the trouble he got himself into, and they forget that there would have been a hell of a scrap right here on the Uncompahgre if we hadn't been on hand to stop it.''

The lieutenant rose, his dark face bitter. ''Take some of those loud-mouthed newspaper editors who keep howling 'The Utes must go.' They cuss Colonel Mackenzie and say he doesn't know anything about Indians and insult him by comparing him to an Army mule and say there's nothing worse than a fool or an Army officer.''

The young officer spat in the fire and swore. ''Why hell, Mackenzie has probably had more Indian fights than any other officer in the Army. He graduated at the head of his class at West Point in 1862. During the war he was brevetted seven times for bravery. He whipped the Cheyennes under Dull Knife, he captured Red Cloud, and he beat hell out of the Comanches in Texas.'' Mills spread his hands in disgust. ''But according to some of the newspapers around here, he's as stubborn as a mule because he won't take advice from them.''

''They're impatient just like the settlers are,'' Mark said, ''so they blame Mackenzie for it.''

''Sure,'' Mills agreed. ''If it had been me, I wouldn't have been as patient as he's been. I know some of the men who were killed up there on Milk Creek under Thornburgh. As far as I'm concerned, a dead Ute is a good Ute, but when you let trouble start, you don't always know where it's going to end. When the commissioners couldn't make the Indians move, they had to turn it over to Mackenzie. He'll move them and it's a good gamble he'll do it without firing a shot.''

Lieutenant Mills turned toward his horse and mounted. "I guess I've talked too much, but I get damned tired of protecting these white bastards who keep kicking us in the butt. Well, I've got to get back to the post. I'll see you in the morning."

"So long," Mark said.

His pipe had gone cold. He knocked it out against his boot heel and sat by the fire for a time listening to the hoofbeats of the lieutenant's horse. He heard him call to Sergeant Maloney and presently the patrol moved downriver past the Agency toward the post.

The campers below him had gone to bed. There was no sound except the soft talk of the river and the lonely call of a coyote from the rim to the west. Mark lay down, his head on his saddle, and stared at the stars and the sky through the thousand leaves of the cottonwood.

He thought first of Laura Engle and was stirred by the warmth of his thoughts, then her father slipped past her, blurring the pictures and turning the warmth to chill despair. What chance was there for a happy marriage with Laura as long as her father was alive? Mark knew as well as he knew anything that no matter where he took her or what they did, the demanding shadow of Will Engle would be upon them.

He thought of his own father and his father's question: Why do men do the things they do to each other? He knew now it was a bigger question than that, a question of what people did to people, of women and children as well as men, and of what nations did to nations. Even worse, it was a question of what a strong nation did to a small and primitive tribe of Indians.

Mark could not agree with Lieutenant Mills that a good Ute was a dead one. He knew them too well for that. He knew, too, that there was something to be said for the Indians in spite of the savage hatred that had exploded on Nathan Meeker and his men at the White River Agency.

Few shared or even understood Mark's feelings on this matter. The editors would go on talking about "Poor Lo" and they'd go on saying "The Utes must go" and Lieutenant Mills could go on thinking the best Ute was a dead one, and the settlers would make their land grab as soon as the Army let them. And what would Mark Manning do, now that he was within hours of having the land he had picked out four years ago? He wasn't sure. He wasn't sure at all.

2

Mark had built his breakfast fire and was filling his coffeepot at the river when he heard horses coming upstream. He got out his bacon and took it and the frying pan to the fire, thinking nothing about the riders who were approaching. He assumed they were two more land seekers from Ouray who had come to find a campsite.

He was kneeling at the fire slicing the bacon when the two men rounded a bend in the road. A moment later he heard Barney Burris's great bellow, "Take a look Dave. It's the deputy and this time he ain't got the girl's skirt to hide behind."

"That's right," Rawlins said. "Think you can take him?"

"Sure I can take him," Burris said. "He ain't got a star on him, neither, like he had in Central City."

Mark rose and faced them, cursing his lack of foresight. His gun and belt lay on the ground beside his saddle and blanket. It had never occurred to him that Rawlins and Burris would show up today, least of all at this early hour. He made one step toward his gun and stopped. Rawlins had drawn his revolver as he had stepped down.

"Leave your iron right where it is," Rawlins said pleasantly. "It wouldn't be much of a fight if you had it in your hand, now would it, Manning? Barney, just to make it fair, suppose you hang your belt over your saddle horn."

"Sure, Dave," Burris said as he swung out of the saddle. "I don't need no hardware for this job."

He unbuckled his gun belt and draped it around his saddle horn, tossed his coat and hat on the ground, and rubbed his palms up and down against his thighs, a wide grin of anticipation on his meaty lips. He was dirty and had not shaved for a week, his stubble as bristly as a wire brush. He moved slowly toward Mark, relishing the whipping he was going to give Mark and not wanting to hurry the moment of pleasure.

Rawlins, as dapper as if he had just finished his morning toilet, asked, "You're mightly slow, Barney. You afraid of him."

Burris snorted in disgust. "Hell no, I ain't afraid of him. No hurry about it that I can see."

Mark backed up, casting a quick glance at his gun and then at the revolver in Rawlins's hand. The only expression he could read on the man's handsome face was the hint of cold amusement in his pale blue eyes. Rawlins would kill him if he made a try for his gun. He was certain of that. He was less certain of how he would come out in a brawl with Burris, but at least he had a chance.

"When Barney gets done with you, Manning," Rawlins said, "Laura Engle won't even look at you. We figured you'd be here by now, not having a wagon to slow you up. You've had this coming from that first day you took a ride with Laura, but we never had a chance to get at you when she wasn't around to see you take your beating. We didn't think she'd want to see it."

"Why don't you try it?" Mark demanded.

Rawlins laughed as if the thought amused him. "Barney wants to do the job. He's very good at this kind of thing, Manning."

"You made one hell of a mistake when you reminded me of that pistol whipping you gave me in Central City," Burris said. "I reckon I'd have remembered it after I seen you a few times, but you hurried it up with your bragging. Now after I stomp your guts out, we'll call it square."

"Get it over with, Barney," Rawlins said impatiently. "If you don't, I will think you're afraid of him. Maybe I'll have to do the job myself."

"The hell you will," Burris snarled, and drove at Mark, his great arms extended as if he intended to hug his enemy to death.

Mark was afraid, as afraid as he had ever been. He knew how Burris fought, he knew the man intended to kill him, or maim him for life so he would be better off dead than alive, and he knew Burris had the physical strength to do it. Then Burris was rushing at him and after that everything he did was prompted by the basic instinct of survival.

Mark made a quarter turn and, raising his elbow, swung it in a savage blow that caught the onrushing Burris in the left eye. He let out a yelp of pain as his head snapped back. He was stopped as sharply as if he had run headlong into a brick wall. Mark was on him immediately, sledging him with powerful blows to his throat just below his chin.

Burris was in agony, made helpless for the moment by his pain. Mark stepped forward and brought his head down so that the top of his skull rammed hard against Burris's nose, smashing it as if it were an overripe plum and bringing a rush of blood that sprayed Mark's face.

"Get him, you fool," Rawlins raged. "Get him down in the dirt. What the hell's the matter with you?"

Half-crazed by pain, Burris got his arms around Mark's waist and tried to wrestle him to the ground. Mark fought to stay on his feet, but Burris had the greater weight and strength. They spilled to the ground and turned over and over again, Burris tightening his grip and squeezing the breath out of Mark.

They rolled again, toward the fire now. Mark's boots hit the coffeepot and upset it, raising a cloud of steam and making a sizzling sound. They went over once more, Burris batting Mark in the face with his skull but never getting in as punishing a blow as Mark had.

Not once did Burris slacken the pressure of his great arms around Mark's body. Mark knew he had to break out of the big man's grip and he didn't have much time left. Every breath was torture and soon he wouldn't even be taking a short breath.

They rolled half over, Mark yanking his right hand free. He jammed him palm hard against Burris's chin and slowly forced his head to one side, fingers and thumb digging into his face. Burris's squeezing grip slackened, not much, but enough to give Mark room to arch his back. He plunged to one side and then the other, gaining a little more room, enough so he was able to smash a knee into Burris's groin. His arms went slack and Mark rolled away and came upright.

Mark had not been aware until that moment of the crowd which had come running from the wagons to watch the fight. He heard a strange, yeasty sigh break out of the

men, and one of them say, "By God, I didn't think he'd
make it."

Burris was on his feet now. He swiped a sleeve across
his battered nose. It came away smeared with blood. Driven
by his implacable hatred, he tottered toward Mark, and
Mark, sensing the necessity of ending it quickly now that
he held an advantage, rushed at Burris. They came together with an audible sound, Burris's arms once more
circling Mark's waist.

Again the big man tried to wrestle Mark to the ground,
but this time the strength was not in him and Mark succeeded in staying on his feet. Burris's face was pressed
against Mark's chest, and now Mark reached out with his
left hand and, grabbing a fistful of Burris's hair, forced the
man's face back and swung his right twice to the other's
jaw, powerful blows that smashed consciousness from him.

Burris's arms slid away from Mark's waist and Mark
stepped back. Burris, unsupported now, went down in a
slow, curling fall and lay motionless on his stomach. Mark
stepped back and took a long, painful breath. It would be
days before the soreness went out of his chest muscles.

"You do that, Rawlins, and I'll shoot you dead right
where you stand."

Mark turned. Rawlins had come up behind him, his
Colt held high. His intention was plain. He had planned
to club Mark to the ground. Lieutenant Mills was the man
who had warned him. He was holding his pistol on Rawlins, and from his expression, Mark guessed he would
have done exactly what he threatened. Rawlins holstered
his gun and turned and walked back to his horse.

"Sergeant." The lieutenant nodded at Sergeant Maloney.
"Have two men move Burris to the river and bring him
around. Then you'll take him and Rawlins to the guardhouse and lock them up for disturbing the peace. If either
man makes a hostile move, shoot him."

"Yes sir," Sergeant Maloney said, a wide grin spreading across his freckled face. "It will be a pleasure, sir."

"You have no right to arrest us, Lieutenant," Rawlins
said. "I'll go to Colonel Mackenzie."

"You do that when you get out of the guardhouse,"
Lieutenant Mills said. "I suppose you're the colonel's

buddy." He put his hands on his hips, his hard stare fixed on Rawlins's face. "I didn't learn anything in Gunnison about who had been selling buckskin, but it strikes me that you and Burris are the kind who would peddle whisky to the Indians and risk a war just for a two-bit payoff. If I could prove it, I wouldn't bother with the guardhouse. I'd shoot you right here."

Rawlins turned and mounted without a word. Sergeant Maloney stood at the river bank with two soldiers who had ducked Burris into the water until he had come around enough to sit up. He sputtered and waved his arms aimlessly while the troopers lifted him to his feet and roughly propelled him to his horse. Another one picked up his hat and coat and shoved it at him. Even after they had heaved him into the saddle, he sat with his head down, still only half aware of what was happening.

Lieutenant Mills motioned to the crowd. "Get back to your wagons. The show's over."

They disappeared. After Sergeant Maloney had moved off with the prisoners, the lieutenant said, "I'll get your fire going and cook you some breakfast. You'll be taking it easy today."

"Just some coffee," Mark muttered and, stumbling to the nearest cottonwood, sat down and leaned against it.

A few minutes later, when the fire was burning and the coffeepot was in place, Jason Mills squatted beside Mark. "I watched the fight from the beginning," he said. "I wasn't going to interfere as long as it was just between you and Burris, but when Rawlins was going to slug with his gun barrel, I decided that was a little too much."

The lieutenant scratched the back of his neck and grinned. "Well, Manning, you are a fighting man. When it started I didn't think you had a show. Seemed like it was matching a greyhound up against a grizzly, but you got the jump on him when you let him have your elbow. He didn't figure on it."

"A hell of a way to fight," Mark said.

"A good way against a man like Burris. Why did they jump you?"

"I arrested Burris once when I was a deputy. He gave me some trouble, so I slugged him with my gun. He's not

one to forget. It's different with Rawlins. He's crazy about
Laura Engle and I'm in his way.''

The lieutenant nodded. "The trouble is I can't keep
them in the guardhouse more than twenty-four hours. They'll
try again.''

Mark nodded. "They'll try again, all right.''

Lieutenant Mills brought him a cup of coffee. He sat
sipping it, wondering what they would try and how soon.

3

The wagons began arriving around noon the following
day, a continuous line that raised a cloud of gray adobe
dust all the way past the Agency to the Army post. Mark
was not surprised that one of the first to appear was Effie
Allen's, Ann Collins on the seat beside her.

Effie had one of the best outfits on the Gunnison, and
Mark had suspected she was one of the best drivers. Now,
watching her wagon wheel pass him, her keen eyes darting
from one side of the road to the other as she looked for a
camping site, he told himself his judgment about her driving ability was right or she wouldn't be among the first to
get here. She'd take care of herself in the run, too, he
thought.

Effie ignored him, but Ann smiled and raised her hand
in a greeting to him. Her blue eyes were red-rimmed from
the dust: it covered her elfin face and her clothes. A lock
of blond hair had struggled loose to flutter above her eyes.
Suddenly conscious of it, she tucked it back into place
under her hat.

She would be an uncommonly pretty girl if she had a
chance to clean up and wear nice clothes and be with
people, but dominated as she was by Effie, she had the
appearance of being so subdued she was barely alive.
Mark felt a great compassion for her. Lieutenant Mills had
been attracted to her, but Mark doubted that even as
redoubtable a man as the lieutenant could get past Effie
long enough to court the girl.

"Did you see the Engle wagons?" he called after them.

"Passed 'em yesterday morning," Effie answered and
went on, not looking back.

He watched them until they reached the end of the valley where the hills pinched in to form the canyon that marked the end of the camping area. Apparently wanting to get closer to the starting line, she swung her team and skillfully put them up the sharp pitch to the bench above Mark. There she made camp.

Lieutenant Mills rode in near the middle of the afternoon. He asked, "How do you feel, Manning?"

Mark grinned wryly. "Stove up a little."

"I had to let them out this morning," the lieutenant said. "I told them to walk easy or I'd lock them up and this time I'd throw away the key. The last I saw of them they were headed back this way."

"I didn't see them," Mark said, "but one thing's sure—I'm not walking off from my gun again."

"They won't try the same thing," the officer said. "I don't take Rawlins for a brawler and Burris has had enough, but when the run starts, you'd better watch out."

"When will that be?"

Lieutenant Mills shrugged. "I don't know. A couple of days. Maybe three. It's up to Colonel Mackenzie. He won't let the settlers move as long as there's a chance the slow Indians might tangle with the fastest whites. Colorow's trying to talk tough, too. We know they've had whisky for some time. Looks like they saved most of it. Now they're drinking. If they've got enough, they'll be ornery."

"I guess Mackenzie can handle them," Mark said.

"Sure he can, but suppose some of the devils got through?" Grimly, the lieutenant waved a hand at the camping settlers. "Think what even a dozen drunk Utes would do?"

"There'd be a hell of a panic," Mark admitted, "but I'll bet Effie Allen wouldn't budge. She'd be the best man of the lot of us."

"Are they here?"

"One of the first." Mark nodded at the bench. "Up there."

"I'll see if they need anything," Lieutenant Mills said, and, reining his horse around, put him up the slope.

He was back in five minutes. "By God, Manning," he exploded, "I have never seen a human being who would make you hate her in as short a time as that bitch. What's the matter with her?''

"I don't know," Mark answered. "I just feel sorry for Ann.''

"So do I," the lieutenant snapped, "and I'm going to do something about it, but I don't know what. I believe Effie would take a shotgun to a man.''

The young Army officer rode upstream, then forded the river and came back on the other side, stopping now and then to talk to a settler. Watching him, Mark thought that if he wasn't transferred, Jason Mills would find out before the winter was over how far Effie would go to keep a man away from Ann. At first Mark had thought of Effie as an overprotective mother hen, but now he decided she was more of a hawk that was inordinately jealous of her adopted child.

He watched for the Engles the rest of that afternoon. The wagons kept coming in a steady stream, spreading out when they reached the camping area so that by evening the only places left were at the base of the mesa hill on the west. Will Engle should have been here hours ago, judging from his position on the Gunnison. He had been closer to the Lake Fork than most of the others. Once he had crossed the stream and climbed the switchbacks to the top of the Blue Mesa, the worst was behind him and he should have kept the same traveling pace as the rest.

Finally with the sun almost down Mark could stand it no longer. He saddled up and rode downstream. When he reached the Agency he saw that the last of the lodges were gone, so the Utes were finally on their way. Unless Colorow made trouble, Colonel Mackenzie would probably let the settlers move day after tomorrow.

The wagons had thinned out until there were only a few scattered ones on the road. Half a mile beyond the Agency Mark met the Engle wagons, Laura riding her bay in front of the first one driven by her father, the second by Charley McGivern.

Mark spoke to Will Engle who gave a sullen, half-inch nod, then he reined in beside Laura. He said, "I got worried about you.''

She didn't answer for a time. She was dusty and tired,

and for some reason which he did not understand, seemed ready to break into tears. Finally she said, "We had a hard time. I'll tell you about it after while."

She was silent, staring straight ahead at the Agency buildings, then she added, "We didn't dream it was such a rough country between here and Gunnison. Then when we had our first look at the valley, I cried. I couldn't help it, Mark. It was so barren and dry with just a few trees along the river. Not even very much sagebrush or greasewood. A lot of it doesn't have anything." She motioned toward the adobe hills to her left. "Like that. Bare. Just bare."

He nodded. "I know. It hit me the same way when I first saw it, but when you get away from the river, or go upstream from here, you'll find some pretty country."

"I keep wondering why people, and this includes me, will go through hardships like this for such an inhospitable land. It isn't worth it, Mark. It isn't worth it."

"It will be in time," he said. "Chances are there'll be a railroad into this valley in a year and people will be pouring in."

"But why, Mark? Why?"

"It's a land of promises," he answered, smiling. "Don't you remember? Cheap land that makes a different promise to each of us."

Laura couldn't smile back. The tears were still too close. She said in a low tone, "It's already broken its promise to me. Maybe I'm as much of a dreamer as Pa, but I pictured the valley as being beautiful, with lots of trees and tall grass and streams of cold, sweet water. It isn't that way at all."

He didn't say anything. There was nothing to say. Reality had destroyed the dream picture she had of the valley. It took a great deal of imagination to project one's thoughts ahead in time and think what the valley would be in twenty years. Or even ten. If Laura could not do it, certainly Will Engle couldn't, either. Mark doubted that the man would stay through the winter.

When they were past the Agency, Mark turned back to ride beside Will Engle's wagon. He said, "All the good camping places are taken. You'll have to swing off the road to the base of the hill." He pointed ahead to the right

of the road. ''You can squeeze in there. It's quite a piece
to the river, but it's the best you can do.''

Engle made a gesture that included all the open country
between the Agency and the river. ''Why hell, there's no
reason why we can't camp here.''

''The Army drew a line and you'll get behind it,'' Mark
said curtly and, touching up his horse, caught up with
Laura.

Will Engle did not believe him just as he had not
believed him when he had asked about the best town site
in the valley. When the time came, he would pick the
wrong spot as he had been doing all his life.

When they were within fifty yards of the line, Engle
called. ''Laura, swing toward the river. We'll camp here.''

''No,'' Mark told her. ''The Army won't let you. Those
wagons you see ahead of you are on the line. You'll have
to find a place behind them. I've already told him, but he
didn't believe me.''

Laura looked at him sharply, then the tears that had
been threating so long rolled down her dust-covered cheeks.
''He doesn't believe anybody until it's too late.''

Wiping her eyes, she rode on with Mark. Her father
called after her as he turned toward the river, McGivern
following. A moment later Sergeant Maloney galloped
toward Engle, shouting, ''No camping there.'' He jerked a
big thumb at the mass of wagons behind him. ''You'll
camp with the rest.''

''The hell I will,'' Engle shouted belligerently. ''There's
plenty of room right here. Why should I get back there
with all that crowd?''

''Because it's where you're supposed to,'' the sergeant
said angrily. ''That's where you'll camp or you're headed
for the guardhouse. Make up your mind, mister. I've got
my orders.''

Mark didn't look back, and he didn't hear anything else
from Engle. When he did glance around several minutes
later, he saw that the two wagons were in the road again.

Laura said sadly, ''That's it, Mark, the same pattern
he's followed all his life. It's why we got behind. Big John
Draper told him to double team up the switchbacks on this
side of the Lake Fork. Pa wouldn't do it because he'd seen

some wagons go on up without double teaming, so he said it would just be a waste of time. What he wouldn't admit was that he had a heavier load than the wagons that were ahead of us.

"He stalled like Draper said he would and that stopped the whole line behind us. He went kind of crazy and I thought he would beat his horses to death. I couldn't stop him. Neither could McGivern. The men behind us were yelling and cursing him until Draper came along. He got Pa calmed down, then he unhooked the team McGivern was driving and with four horses pulling, he drove to the top, then he took the horses back and McGivern brought the second wagon up."

She paused, choking on the bitterness of the memory. Then she said, "After that the other wagons passed us whenever they could. Sometimes they almost forced us off the road. You never saw such mean looks as they gave Pa. They hate him, Mark. What's worse, they despise him. They'll starve before they'll buy anything at his store."

"They'll forget in time," he said.

"I won't," she said instantly. "I never will."

Mark said nothing then. There was nothing to say. She had her pride and she had been humiliated by her father for no sensible reason. Call it bad judgment or just plain stupidity, but whatever it was in Will Engle's makeup, there was no excuse for it.

He angled off the road toward the mesa hill, Laura riding beside him. Engle and McGivern followed. When they reached an open area big enough for a campsite, Mark stepped down and gave Laura a hand. When she was on her feet, she closed her eyes, one hand on the saddle horn to steady herself. She was so tired, he thought, that she was close to fainting.

Mark didn't move until Engle and McGivern had unhooked and taken the horses to the river to be watered. Then he held Laura's hands in his as he said, "You can't go on giving up for him, Laura. He's like a little boy who's got to learn to walk by himself. You deserve something better. Maybe I can't give you what you deserve, but let me try. Marry me, Laura. I love you very much."

Her lips parted as she stared at him, and then her

self-control broke and he put his arms around her and she
cried, her face buried against his chest. Then she lifted her
face to be kissed, and she whispered, "Mark, Mark, I've
wanted so much to hear you say that. I think I loved you
the first night when we walked together, or during our ride
the next day."

"Then you will marry me?"

"Of course, Mark. Any day. Any time."

"Then we'd better tell your Pa now," he said, and she
nodded.

He led her horse to the river, and when he returned, he
saw that Engle and McGivern were back with the teams
and Laura had told her father.

"So you're fixing to get married," Engle said to him
sullenly. "I seen it coming right from the first. Well, I
told you I don't know nothing about you. I still don't. All
I've got to say is you'd better be good to her."

"I'll do that without your threats," Mark said.

Engle chewed on his lower lip, not liking it as Mark
knew he wouldn't, but whether it was because he didn't
want to give Laura up or whether he was afraid of Dave
Rawlins was a question in Mark's mind. Perhaps it was
some of both.

"All right," Engle said finally. "Go ahead and get
married, but I'm asking one thing. Wait till I get the store
started. I'll need her that long."

Because Laura was who she was and what she was with
a compelling sense of duty, she said, "Yes, Mark, we can
wait that long."

Mark nodded, not wanting to argue with Laura at this
moment, but knowing that if he wasn't careful, Will Engle
would convince Laura he needed her as long as he lived.
The terrible truth was he would.

6

Ann Collins

1

Effie Allen brought two buckets of water from the river. Ann heated part of one in a pan and, stepping into the wagon, took a sponge bath and changed her clothes. Still she felt as if the dust was in her mouth and nose and ears and she wondered if she would ever feel completely clean again.

She cooked supper, ignoring Effie who sat by the fire, her eyes half-closed as if trying to make a decision. Ann had not spoken to her since she had curtly and rudely sent Lieutenant Mills about his business.

It was just one more link in the long chain of injustices she had suffered at Effie's hands, and she was resolved it would be the last. For the first time she realized she hated Effie. She would leave her as soon as she found something to do. In a new country like this, it should not be difficult.

After supper Effie took care of the horses and Ann cleaned up the dishes, then Effie returned to the fire. It was dusk now, and Ann decided there must be more than one hundred campfires around them, with all the noise and excitement that came from so many people being crowded together. They were visiting back and forth. Children were shouting and running from one wagon to another. A group of young people had gathered by the river and were singing. In spite of all this, Effie somehow contrived to live as if she and Ann were alone and no one else was within fifty miles of them.

Ann stood on one side of the fire staring at Effie. She had not intended to say anything about the way Effie had treated Lieutenant Mills. They had said it all before at one time or another, and there was no use repeating it. The

difference was that before this Ann had remembered those
terrible hours in Pueblo when it seemed as if there was no
hope for her. Now she was not afraid. She thought she
knew the reason. If she was ever to have a husband and
children, she had to start living her own life.

She opened her mouth to say she was going to leave as
soon as Effie was settled on her claim, but she didn't get it
said. Effie rose and said, now that she had made a decision
and everything was settled, "I'm taking a walk. Don't ask
me where I'm going. If you don't know, you can't tell
anybody. I may not get back tonight, so don't worry about
me."

She dropped some biscuits into a flour sack, then turned
to Ann. "Now you take care of the horses if I'm not back
by daylight. Feed 'em good cause I don't want 'em ganted
up when we make the run."

Without another word she walked around the wagon and
threaded her way through the neighboring camps, moving
toward the mesa hill to the west. Ann watched her until
she lost her in the rapidly thinning light. Effie had stopped
the wagon when they'd had their first good look at the
valley as they'd come down Cedar Creek that morning
and, taking out her glasses, had carefully studied the river,
the land on both sides, and the mesa on the west.

Without a word she put away the glasses and drove on.
She didn't say so, but Ann was sure she had picked out the
spot she wanted. If she didn't get there first, she would
probably jump the claim. It would be like her, and Ann
was convinced there wasn't a man among the settlers who
was capable of fighting her off.

Ann turned to the fire. That was when the daring plan
came to her, so daring it shocked her and made her
breathless. *She could take a claim of her own.*

This was the one way she could show Effie she was a
person with rights and desires and ambitions of her own.
She had never known Effie to make a mistake, but as
confident as she was of her own judgment, she might
make one now. If she did, and if Ann had the good land,
Effie would come to her and she would have an advantage
for the first time since she had started living with Effie.

She walked quickly toward the river, more excited than she had ever been in her life. Mark Manning had the answer for her. She judged him to be a kind man, and so he would certainly tell her what she needed to know.

She found him finishing supper. She saw that he was surprised at her visit. She said quickly, "I just wanted to talk to you for a minute, Mr. Manning. Effie's gone and I was lonesome."

"Draw up a chair and sit down," he said. "Have a cup of coffee?"

"No thank you. I just had supper." She took a long breath. "Mr. Manning, Mr. Draper told me you used to work on the reservation."

He nodded. "I worked here about a year."

"Mr. Draper said you said that some of the land was poor and some was good and you knew where to go for good land. Will you tell me were it is? Please?"

He didn't answer for a time. He took out his pipe and filled and lighted it, and after he had puffed a few times, he said, "I don't want you to think I'm altogether selfish, although I may be. It's this way. If I told you and you told somebody else and it spread all over camp, I wouldn't have much chance of getting the land I wanted. There would be a stampede. As it is, I won't have any trouble. Not much anyhow. I suppose there are a few men in the bunch who know the reservation as well as I do, but there wouldn't be many."

She asked, her voice no more than a whisper, "Then you won't tell me?"

"I'm sorry, Miss Collins." He took his pipe out of his mouth and smiled at her. "There's another thing, too. You'd make a fine neighbor, but I couldn't stand living beside your partner."

Ann whirled and ran back up the slope to Effie's camp. Effie's horses. Effie's food. Even her dresses had been bought by Effie. She couldn't go on living this way. She just couldn't. Maybe Dave Rawlins would help her. Or that nice Lieutenant Mills. But she knew she couldn't bring herself to ask either one of them.

That night she cried herself to sleep.

2

Effie did not return during the night. Ann slept later than usual. After she woke she lay on her back, staring at the canvas above her. She should get up and feed and water the horses and build a fire and cook her breakfast. If Effie returned and found her lolling in bed this way, she'd take the hide right off her back.

It was very late by Effie's standards when Ann got up and dressed and stepped out of the wagon to face a hostile world which seemed to have no room for her. She led the horses to the river, angling downstream so she would avoid Mark Manning. She still wondered if she'd had a nightmare and hadn't really asked him where the good land was. She'd counted on him and he had refused to answer one simple question which meant so much to her. But it was no nightmare. He had refused to answer, so there was no use to ask again.

After she took care of the horses, she started a fire and cooked breakfast. She sat beside it with a tin cup of coffee in her hand, hearing the sounds of visiting at other wagons, the talking and the laughter, but no one came to see her. Not that she expected anyone to come. By this time probably everyone in camp knew about Effie.

When she heard a man say, "May the Lord show you His smiling face, Miss Ann," she was so startled she almost dropped her cup. Big John Draper had stepped over the tongue of the wagon and was standing beside the front wheel, leaning on his staff and smiling at her.

"Good morning, Mr. Draper," she said. "I was surprised to see you. Nobody ever comes to visit us. Effie drives them off when they do come, so they quit coming."

He walked to the fire and sat down across from her, laying his staff on the ground beside him. He said sympathetically, "I have noticed that, Miss Ann. She is terribly wrong. Whether you like people or not, they are in the world with us and we have to live with them."

She was silent a moment, thinking that was exactly the way she felt, but Effie didn't and Effie wasn't going to change. Then she remembered her manners and asked, "Can I give you a cup of coffee, Mr. Draper?"

"I would be glad to share your coffee," he said.

She poured a cup and handed it to him. He had a friendly face. He must, she thought, be a very holy man judging from the selfless way he lived. Effie's wagon had been next to Will Engle's wagons when they had stalled on the switchbacks above the Lake Fork and she had seen what John Draper had done. As far as she could tell, Engle had not even thanked him for his help.

"Where is Miss Effie?" Draper asked.

"She left last night," Ann answered. "She didn't say where she was going."

"She must be on the reservation somewhere spying out the land," Draper said. "It is unfortunate because the Army is throwing everyone into the guardhouse that it catches doing that."

"It would serve her right," Ann said with great violence.

He looked at her in surprise, for she seldom spoke with any strong feeling. He said mildly, "Do you really mean that, Miss Ann?"

"Yes." She looked at him for a long moment, thinking how much he looked like one of the Apostles, perhaps Peter who had been a fisherman and therefore must have been a strong man like Draper. Then, because she sensed the sympathy and understanding and kindness that was in him, she said, "Mr. Draper, I've got to talk to someone. Will you listen?"

"Of course, Miss Ann."

The words poured out of her, the story back as far as her mother's death and that horrible, hopeless interlude in Pueblo, and her life with Effie and how Effie in her possessive way drove people off, and finally how that she had thought of taking up a claim of her own and Mark Manning had refused to tell her where to go.

"Don't you see, Mr. Draper?" she said. "If this is the way Effie wants to live, she can, but I can't. I've been a terrible coward or I'd have made a change before now. If I can't take my own land, I've got to find someone to work for."

"I'm sure you can," he said.

"I want my own home," she went on. "I want a husband and children. I want my own family. Is there anything wrong with that?"

"No," he said. "They are the natural things for a normal woman to want, but until the country is settled, it will be hard for you to find work. For a little while longer you had better stay with Miss Effie. Meanwhile, as I visit among the people, I'll see if I can find a place for you."

She heard horses and looked up just as Dave Rawlins and Barney Burris rode around the rear of the wagon. She rose, her heart dancing as she looked at Rawlins. She had allowed herself to daydream about him, and at the same time she had been afraid he would never come back to see her, yet here he was and on the one day when Effie was gone.

"Good morning, Mr. Rawlins," she said. "Won't you get down?"

She ignored Barney Burris. She was uneasy in his presence. She didn't know what there was about him, but whenever she was around him, she had the same feeling she had when she saw a lizard or snake or toad. She did not understand, either, why a man like Dave Rawlins had anything to do with Barney Burris.

"Thank you." Rawlins lifted his hat in his usual gallant manner. "I'll be glad to visit a while."

He dismounted and walked toward the fire, glancing at Draper who was on his feet and leaning on his staff, staring at Rawlins, his face reflecting his distrust of the man. Burris remained in the saddle, his gaze moving from Ann to Draper.

"Take a walk, old man," Burris ordered. "Your visiting time is up."

"No," Draper said firmly. "You will not bluff me as you have so many. The stench of evil is upon both of you. Ride off and leave the girl alone."

"Well now," Burris said as he swung to the ground. "That's tough talk coming from a sky pilot. Let's see if you can make it stand up."

"Leave us alone," Ann cried. "Mr. Rawlins, he's your friend. Send him away."

Rawlins shook his head, smiling. "I'm sorry, but there are times when he just won't listen to me."

Burris walked slowly toward Draper, his intent plain. Draper didn't back up, but Ann, glancing at him, saw that he was frightened and she knew that he had reason to be. She ran to Burris and grabbed an arm.

"Don't touch him," she cried. "Don't you dare touch him. Go away. He didn't hurt you."

Burris jerked free, a violent thrust of his big arm that sent her spinning. He took two more steps, and then, ten feet from the preacher, he stopped as Mark Manning said, "You touch him, Burris, and I'll kill you." He nodded at Rawlins. "You might get me while I'm doing it, but if you do, the lieutenant will throw you back into the guardhouse and lose the key."

Ann cried out, an incoherent sound of relief. Mark Manning stood motionless at the edge of the bench, right hand close to the butt of his gun. He was smiling slightly, almost contemptuously as if he hoped Rawlins or Burris or both would try for their guns.

She had always thought of Rawlins as a Prince Charming, a good and handsome knight who by nature belonged to King Arthur's Round Table. Now, knowing as little as she did about men, she still recognized the expression of feral hatred that twisted and darkened Rawlins's face, then it was gone, and she felt as if she had just looked into the man's heart, that John Draper had been right when he'd said the stench of evil was on both men.

"I'll call again, Miss Collins," Rawlins said. "Come on, Barney. We'll see Manning again, too."

They mounted and rode away. Draper said, "He would have beaten me badly, I think."

"Yes, I believe he would have," Manning said. "I recognized their voices. That's why I poked my nose into the business. I had a fight with Burris yesterday and I whipped him, so now he's looking for somebody else he can take his meanness out on. You happened to be the first he had a chance at."

"Thank you," Draper said. "I'd better stay with Miss Ann. I don't think they'll come back, and I don't suppose I could do much good against Burris if they did, but perhaps I'll be some company to her."

After Manning left, Ann looked at Draper and shook her head, the tears threatening. This was the first real gesture of friendly concern that anyone except Effie had made toward her for a long time. "Thank you, Mr. Draper," she said. "Thank you very much."

"It's my pleasure," he said gently. "I'll stay till Miss Effie returns."

7

Mark Manning

1

Shortly before six o'clock that evening Lieutenant Jason Mills arrived from the Army post, said something to Sergeant Maloney, and then the sergeant rode along the line, bellowing, "You'll be permitted to go onto the reservation at five o'clock in the morning at the sound of the bugle."

The news spread back to the rear of the camp in a matter of seconds. Some of the men cheered, others muttered, "It's about time," and a few yelled derisively, "Who's scared the worst, you or the Injuns?"

So the moment was here at last, Mark thought as he watched Lieutenant Mills ride toward him, a moment that had been in his mind even when he had worked on the reservation. It had been plain enough to the honest man even then that the Utes would go, for this was land white men could use. Naturally a conquered people would not be permitted to keep it. The question was one of time. All the whites needed was an excuse, and the White River Utes gave it to them when they murdered Nathan Meeker and every man who worked at the Agency.

At 5 A.M. Mark would ride with the others and stake out

a claim of one hundred and sixty acres of land. His father, if he knew what was happening, would ask as he had so many times: Why do men do the things they do to each other? After all this time Mark still had no answer.

The lieutenant reined up at Mark's camp and dismounted. He said, "Well, we finally got the word. I suppose you're as impatient as the rest."

Mark grinned. "Why, no, Lieutenant. I'm a very patient man."

Lieutenant Mills studied him a moment to determine if he was being facetious, then said, "I'm not. I'm glad to get it over with, and without bloodshed. It was touch and go for a while, though. Colorow and his bunch have been damned ugly. I told you they had some whisky. Well, we had a few friendlies who kept us informed on what was happening. Colorow told the young bucks they'd whipped Thornburgh and they'd killed the men at the White River Agency, and he said they could do the same here.

"I guess he convinced them because they came riding up the valley hell for leather, all painted up like a bunch of devils. There was a lot of them and they made a sight, I tell you, but Colonel Mackenzie was ready for them. He had his men lined up across the valley with his cannons on the bluffs on both sides. If the Indians had kept coming, we'd have blown them to pieces, but when they saw how things stacked up, they lost their courage and didn't fire a shot. They just turned around and went back, but old Colorow pulled up and looked at us like he had a notion to try it singlehanded. Some say he's all bluff and a coward, but he was the last to turn around."

"I guess Mackenzie knew what he was doing," Mark said.

"Sure he did," Mills said indignantly, "but these newspaper editors sitting back in their safe little offices kept saying he didn't know anything about Indians. If the colonel hadn't been ready for them and they'd got this far, the Uncompahgre would have run red for a week." The lieutenant's dark face turned thoughtful. "But there was a funny thing happened. Once the Utes got on the move, they traveled pretty well, and with a lot of stock, too, but first they lay down on the ground and kissed it and flung out their arms as if they were trying to embrace it, then they got up and went on, some of them crying.''

Mills scratched the back of his neck, scowling as he tried to sort out his thoughts. "The thing is, Manning, I've always hated Indians. A lot of Army men do. Maybe most of us. I've fought the Comanches in Texas and the Apaches in New Mexico and Arizona, and I've seen what they do to white women and children on ranches that were unprotected. I guess I never really thought of them as human beings before. Not until today.''

"It's a common mistake," Mark said. "The trouble is not many of us put ourselves in their place, but if we were fighting for our homes, we might not act very human either.''

"Maybe we wouldn't," the lieutenant agreed as he turned to his horse.

"Will Engle disappeared last night," Mark said. "Have you got him in the guardhouse?''

The officer turned, scowling. "I'm damned if I know, but we've got a bunch of them. If a man's so greedy he can't wait for the law to let him onto the reservation, it's my judgment he doesn't deserve any consideration.''

"You won't get an argument out of me on that," Mark said, "but there's something else. Effie Allen is gone, too. Maybe you've got a women in with all those men.''

Lieutenant Mills cursed, then suddenly he grinned. "Wouldn't that be hell in a bucket? It could happen at that, I guess, as much as she looks and acts like a man." Then his face turned grave. "What about Ann?''

Mark told him about his trouble with Burris and Rawlins that morning, and added, "John Draper is staying with her, but maybe you ought to talk to her. She tried to get me to tell her where I was going to settle, but I wouldn't. I don't want to have anything to do with that Effie woman. It's different with Ann and I feel sorry for her. I think she's afraid. Afraid of Effie and still afraid to break loose from her.''

"That bitch," Mills muttered as he stepped into the saddle. "All right, I'll stop and tell Ann to let me know if Burris or Rawlins bothers her any more." He paused, frowning, then he said, "You know, Manning, I like Ann.

I haven't seen much of her, either. Maybe it's just like you said. A man naturally feels sorry for her, with that damned Effie telling her when to take in a breath and when to let it out again.''

"That's part of it," Mark said, "but there's something else that worries me. When a girl like Ann finally gets pushed too far, she's going to turn to somebody for help. It might be Rawlins. He's the kind who appeals to some women."

"Then I'll kill him," the lieutenant said. "She's just a child, and if he takes advantage of her, I tell you, I'll kill him."

He rode up the slope to the bench. A few minutes later when Mark walked past Ann's camp, he saw that Mills was squatting beside the fire drinking coffee with her and John Draper. A lot had happened to Ann today, he thought as he strode on to the Engle camp, good as well as bad, and more would happen if the girl could free herself from Effie's dominating will.

Laura had asked Mark to have supper with them. When he reached their camp, he saw that Will Engle had not returned. He nodded at Charley McGivern and asked Laura how she felt.

"Better than yesterday," she said. "At least I'm rested." She shook her head and smiled. "The truth is I'm a little scared of tomorrow."

"If your pa doesn't get back, I'll drive for you," he said.

"No, Mark," she said sharply. "You have your own future to look after. I mean, ours. It's not your fault that Pa sashays off and gets arrested."

"It's not yours, either." Mark motioned to the wagons. "You can't race with anybody. They're too heavy. It's crazy."

"We're not going to race," she said. "I can drive a team as well as anybody and I'll get there. That's all Pa wants. McGivern will take the other one. We know the place. It's not far down the river. Pa thinks everybody will go farther down, so maybe we won't have any trouble."

He knew her too well to argue with her. Will Engle was her cross and she refused to let him help her bear it.

Sometimes he despaired when he thought about it and wondered if the day would ever come when he and Laura would be married.

After they had eaten, he said, "I'll get on back so you can go to bed. You sleep as much as you can the first part of the night because nobody is going to sleep much the last half."

"I'll try," she said, and when he held his arms out to her, she ran into them and hugged him with a fierce possessiveness she had not shown him before. She whispered, "I know I shouldn't worry about Pa, but I can't help it."

"He's a grown man," Mark said, "and he refuses to accept advice from anyone. We can't do anything for him."

"I know, I know," she said. "I keep telling myself that. Sometimes I think I hate him so much I've got to go off and never see him again, but I can't, Mark. I just can't."

He kissed her once more and whispered, "Be careful tomorrow."

As he walked away, he told himself that Will Engle was his cross, too, whether Laura wanted it to be or not.

2

Mark slept about two hours before midnight, and after that there was no use to try to sleep. The earth became alive with noise: people packing and breaking camp, the rattle of trace chains and the squeal of leather as men moved up to the line, curses and angry voices and now and then Sergeant Maloney's bellowed threat to throw a man into the guardhouse even at this late hour if he didn't back up to where he belonged.

Mark loaded his pack animal and saddled his horse, and with more than an hour to go, mounted and rode up the steep slope to the bench. Effie's wagon loomed high and dark in the moonlight, but there was no fire, and he did not see either the horses or Ann and John Draper. He wondered about them, and whether Effie had returned, and then put them out of his mind.

He found that McGivern had harnessed the Engle horses, and he and Laura had edged forward so they had their positions near the end of the line. He saw Laura's vague shape beside the front wheel and he called to her before he rode up. She turned, answering, and he dismounted and stood beside her, an arm around her waist.

"Lieutenant Mills rode by a few minutes ago," Laura said. "He wondered where you were."

"I'm not in as big a hurry as most of them," he said.

"Greed," she said bitterly. "I wonder how many millionaires will be made today."

"I doubt if any are," he said. "Nobody will have title to their land until it's surveyed. That'll be a year. Maybe two. By that time probably not more than ten per cent of the people who are making the run today will still be here."

"Pa won't," she said. "That will be a safe bet."

There was some jockeying for position somewhere along the line, then curses and the sound of blows. A trooper appeared at once and separated the two men and asked if they wanted to see Lieutenant Mills or Sergeant Maloney. Both settlers declined, and then there was silence as the dawn light deepened. The sky seemed to be clear. It would be a hot day, Mark thought, a day to remember, this third day of September, 1881.

Now and then a match flared as someone looked at his watch. A neighbor would ask the time and be answered. Forty minutes yet. Thirty-five minutes. Then thirty, each minute dragging out. A trooper appeared out of the gloom, rode past in front of Laura and Mark and turned and rode back. Now the tension was a tangible pressure that seemed almost unbearable, and Mark thought how the hopes and dreams of these people must be building in their minds.

Ten minutes, then five. Men were in saddles, or the seats of buggies and carts, tense-muscled as they waited out these last, endless minutes. Get ahead of their neighbors, they were thinking. There were rich prizes waiting for the swift today. Good farms. Stock ranches. And to the astute merchant and town promoter, there were town sites to be occupied and held by force until they could be developed later.

Mark kissed Laura, whispering again for her to be careful, and gave her a hand up to her seat. He stepped into the saddle and waited, then it came, the sharp, clear tone of the bugle knifing into the early morning air.

The boomers were off like a race at a country fair, the horsemen out in front, the buggies and carts careening behind, and a few loaded wagons groaning and creaking as their wheels rolled over the sagebrush toward the road. They would take what the others didn't want.

He waited until he saw that Laura's wagon had reached the road. Satisfied then that she would be all right, he turned and rode up the mesa hill through the scattered piñons and cedars until he reached the top.

Here was a road that had been cut through the pygmy forest. It was used by freighters when the river was too high to cross or when the valley road was mudded up so badly it was practically impassable. Gradually the sun rose and heat began settling down upon the valley. An hour later he could clearly see the adobe hills on the other side of the river, and watch the dust rise from the road. Already some of the horsemen were far past the Agency. Soon they would reach the Army post.

He was not sure when he was aware he was being followed. At first it was no more than a vague stirring along his spine, perhaps stemming from the suspicion he'd had since his fight with Burris that the big man and Rawlins would be on his trail today. Here was the best possible opportunity for murder, with almost everybody below him in the valley and the chances of meeting anyone else on this lonely road close to zero.

He looked back often. Whenever he reached a straight stretch in the road, he would stop at the north end and wait, but no one appeared. Imagination, he decided. Nothing more. It was like picking a tick off your body in the spring, and after that you were crawling all over with the feeling that you were covered by them.

Then, just before the road dropped off the mesa to curve toward the valley road, he saw clearly a fine trace of dust behind him. He took a long breath, knowing that this was more than imagination. If he had to fight Burris and Rawlins today, he would rather do it face to face than run the chance of being shot in the back. He reined off into a cedar thicket and drew his gun and waited.

It seemed a long time before he saw them. When he did, he sucked in a whistling breath and began to curse. His pursuers were Ann Collins and John Draper. He holstered his gun and, mounting his horse, waited in the road for them.

"So you're bound to live beside me, are you, Miss Collins?" he asked when they reached him.

They were riding Effie's horses bareback. Ann looked straight at him, her shoulders back, her trim breasts held high and proud, and she said with more defiance than he thought she possessed, "I will if I can, Mr. Manning, but it's not because I'm so fond of you. I want good land. Effie never came back to the wagon, so she may not get any land. If she doesn't, she may want to live with me. Don't you see, Mr. Manning? I've got to be right just once."

He understood. There was more to it than he had thought. He looked at Draper who shook his head. "No, I'm not taking a claim. I told Miss Ann I would stay with her today and look out for her as much as I could."

"All right, come along," Mark said curtly as he pointed to the mesa ahead. "We ride to the top and we work our way through the cedars and piñons the best we can. There's no road. It's a long ways yet and you won't be able to walk tomorrow."

"I'll manage it somehow," Ann said. "I've got to, Mr. Manning. I've just got to."

"Maybe you don't know it," Mark said, "but you had me scared. I thought Rawlins and Burris were on my tail."

"They are," Draper said.

"You sure?"

"I'm sure. I had a good look at them once when the cedars thinned out. I have very good distance vision, Mr. Manning."

"Then we'd best get moving," Mark said.

He led out, wondering with wry amusement how he managed to collect helpless girls and old preachers the way he did.

8

Laura Engle

1

Laura made no attempt to race with the heavily loaded wagon. She was the last to reach the road, having to start from the base of the mesa hill. Charley McGivern was somewhere ahead of her. She could not see him, for the dust from dozens of vehicles and horses was drifting back toward her. She could do nothing except bow her head and hold the team to its plodding pace.

Undoubtedly her father was in the guardhouse at the Army post. She had no idea when he would be released. She had not mustered enough courage to ask Lieutenant Mills about it. Perhaps he would never know her father had been arrested. It was just as well he didn't.

This was so much like Will Engle. He could not take his chances with everyone else, but he had to try to maneuver into a position of advantage to himself. As usual, he wound up worse off than if he had started with the rest. It had been foolish. He had no reason to explore the reservation because he had already picked out the spot he wanted when they had passed the Army post on their way in.

She lifted her head and noticed that she was past the Agency. The dust was not so bad now. The boomers had scattered out, the riders on fast horses moving far ahead of anyone else, the buggies and carts well down the road past the Agency. Only the other heavy wagons were directly ahead of her, moving at about the same plodding gait she was taking, dust stirred by hoofs and wheels.

Perhaps, as her father had said, the settlers would keep going and pass up the good locations at this end of the valley. They had seen part of the country as they had come in. It would be like them, she thought, to push on into the unknown, driven by the hope that whatever lay ahead would be better than what they had seen. Later some might come back and locate on land they had passed up today, but by that time her father would have his claim. Or if he was still in the guardhouse, she and Charley McGivern would hold it until he was released.

In any case, there was plenty of good land here on the Uncompahgre for everyone who had taken part in the run. The valley was wider farther downstream and it ran for miles along the river, Mark had said, even past the junction of the Gunnison and the Uncompahgre.

Too, there was the long line of mesas to the west. She wondered what it was like on top of those tablelands and if that was where Mark had gone. He hadn't offered to tell her and she hadn't asked. She wanted him to feel she trusted his judgment completely, and yet she did not share his enthusiasm for the valley. She had hated it the moment she had seen it, the hot sun glaring on the barren adobe soil with its scattered sage and chico brush.

She glanced at the adobe hills to her right and shuddered as she turned her head. They were utterly repulsive to her, so bare of vegetation that they looked as if the Lord had cast a blight upon them. She wasn't sure she could spend a lifetime here even with Mark. No, that was wrong, she told herself immediately. She could live anywhere with Mark. The problem was living the hours and days and perhaps weeks before they were married.

This thought brought her mind to Will Engle. If anything happened that kept her from marrying Mark . . . something that made it impossible for her to leave her father . . . She couldn't stand it if that happened, she told herself miserably. She just couldn't. There had been too much of that kind of living back to the day her mother had died. The time comes when anyone reaches the end of his or her capacity to give, even a daughter. She had reached that point.

2

Laura had been driving more than two hours and was just beyond the Army post when she saw the first stake

with the white rag fluttering at the top. The stake marked
the corner of someone's claim. Belatedly she realized this
was the land her father wanted. Either he was out of the
guardhouse or McGivern had located the corner for him.

She drove on, eyes searching for her father or McGivern,
or at least the other wagon, but she did not see them.
Then, a moment later, she rounded a curve in the river and
saw a man standing beside a buggy, a rifle in his hand.
He was a big and raw-boned man with a ragged beard and
small, red-flecked eyes. She had seen him on the Gunnison,
but she had never talked to him and did not know his name.

The man watched her, not moving until she came opposite him and stopped. He stepped away from his buggy as
he jerked his head downstream and pointed the rifle at her.
He said, "Keep moving, ma'am."

"Who are you?" she demanded.

"Whit Bailey, if it's any of your business. This is my
claim and I sure ain't letting anybody jump it, so just keep
them wheels rolling."

Traveling fast in his buggy, he must have reached here
long before McGivern had and then he'd probably told
McGivern to keep moving just as he was telling Laura.
Her father by his lawless act of sneaking onto the reservation ahead of time had made this possible. He could have
ridden Fox, who was tied behind the wagon, or she could
have, and got here ahead of Whit Bailey and held this
piece of land until the wagons arrived.

Will Engle's big plans had failed again, and suddenly
she was angry. She cried. "This claim was to be my
father's . . ."

"But it ain't. It's mine." Bailey grinned and spat a
brown stream at the nearest clump of sagebrush. "He had
a real good idea, settling here and having a store and selling
whisky to the soljers. Trouble is, he talked too much
afore he left the Gunnison, and I kinder cottoned to his
notion, so you just keep moving, ma'am. This is my land
and I ain't letting Will Engle or nobody else have it."

She drove on. There was nothing else she could do. She
wondered what her father would do when he got out of the
guardhouse. His heart had been set on having this land, on
starting a store close to the post. He might try to jump the

claim, and if he did, Whit Bailey would probably kill him. He had the look of that kind of man.

Maybe she should go to the guardhouse and talk to her father. She had to convince him he shouldn't do anything rash. Perhaps she could see Lieutenant Mills. He couldn't do anything about getting the claim away from Bailey, but at least he could try to talk some sense into Will Engle's head.

She was still thinking about it when she reached the other wagon half an hour later. It had been pulled off the road next to the river. She did not see her father until she stepped down and walked toward McGivern who was leaning against a rear wheel and placidly chewing tobacco as if this was just an ordinary day and nothing had happened.

Will Engle was sitting on a flat rock near the bank. One eye was shut and the left corner of his mouth was bruised and swollen. She cried, "Pa, did the soldiers do that?"

He didn't answer for a moment. His face reflected his utter misery. Finally he said, "No, Laura. The soldiers didn't catch me. I hid all day yesterday here along the river. Several patrols rode by within twenty feet of me, but they didn't spot me. Soon as it was daylight this morning I was up and had the stakes in and the white rags tied around 'em afore the first rider went by, then Whit Bailey came along."

Engle swallowed and turned his good eye away from Laura. "I'd gabbed too much and he'd heard me and figured it was a good idea to have a store in this end of the valley. He stopped his buggy and walked up to me and hit me in the mouth and knocked me down. I got up and he hit me in the eye and knocked me down again."

"You had your gun," Laura cried. "Why didn't you defend your claim?"

"I never got a chance to use it," he said defensively. "He got me by the collar and the seat of my pants and marched me about fifty feet and then kicked me so hard I fell down. He said to keep going till I got past my north stake or he'd shoot me. I did. I was just sitting here when Charley came along."

He did not look at her. He must know, she thought, how she felt, how that this was a repetition of the same old pattern she had seen so many times since her mother had died. Only this time it was different because her money had brought them here, her money had bought the teams and wagons and had paid for the merchandise that was in the wagons.

She said, "I'll untie Fox and see if I can find Mark. You won't need me any more."

"You can't do that." Engle rose and motioned to the land that lay to the west and north. "We'll claim our land right here. We're still pretty close to the post and we'll have our store just as we figured. There's a fine grove of trees here, better'n the ones Bailey got. We'll cut some of 'em and we'll put up a store building right away and you'll have your tent just like you had on the Gunnison. You'll be real comfortable."

She turned away from him and walked toward her horse. He ran after her and caught her by her arms. "Laura, you promised you wouldn't marry him until the store was going. You promised. Don't you remember?"

She stared at him, loathing him and his weakness and his cowardice and his continual dependence upon her. Then she wondered why she had tried to fool herself, for she had known all the time this was the way it would be because it was the way it had always been. She remembered Mark saying, "He's like a little boy who's got to learn to walk by himself."

He was shaking her roughly and saying, "You promised, Laura. You promised."

She thought, God, will he ever learn to walk by himself? Must I always be here for him to lean upon?

She looked past her father to the far summit of Storm King where the black clouds were gathering. But the answer was not up there and God would not give her the answer. The only answer she would ever find was in her own heart.

"All right, Pa," she said. "I'll keep my promise."

She saw relief flow cross his face. He turned to McGivern. "Come on, Charley. Let's find some stakes and get our corners down before somebody comes along."

She watched him walk away, the big dream glowing before his eyes again, but it was a small reward for what she was giving up.

9

Mark Manning

1

Mark reached his destination before noon. He stepped down and dug his boot toe through the red soil and picked up a handful. He let it dribble out of his hand, the breeze carrying the dust downslope from him, then he turned to Ann and gave her a hand. She slid off the horse and held to him for a moment, swaying so that for a time he thought she was going to faint.

"It's no picnic," he said, "riding this far bareback."

"It certainly isn't." She drew her hand from his and looked around, and even as tired as she was, she seemed completely satisfied with what she saw. "It's beautiful here, Mr. Manning, just beautiful."

Draper had slid off the other horse and was standing beside Ann. "Yes, it is beautiful," he said. "I don't pretend to be an agricultural expert, but I know enough about soils to be sure this is far superior to that which is along the river. I don't suppose anyone would believe it if he didn't see it himself, though. From down there on the river you just don't know how it looks up here on top of the mesa."

Mark turned and walked away, wanting to be by himself for a moment. In a way he felt as if he had come home. He strode beside the creek that talked its way past willow-covered banks, thinking he was here first and so would have prior rights to the water. Ann and a dozen others would have the same rights, but there was not enough water to irrigate the entire top of the mesa, so it was important to be among the first.

Now, looking around, he told himself that it took a good deal of imagination to change this sage-covered land to lush meadows and hay fields; it would take months and years of sweat and hard work to make that dream a reality. The price would be too great for some of the boomers to pay, but not for Mark Manning.

Thirty miles to the north was Grand Mesa, the biggest flat-topped mountain in the world, or so Mark had heard. It had been one of the Utes' favorite hunting grounds, he knew, and from here it gave the appearance of a great ruler laid against the sky. To the west was the Uncompahgre Plateau, its crest forming almost as level a line as Grand Mesa. It was the divide between the San Miguel and Uncompahgre rivers.

To the south were the San Juans, with the so-called Sawtooth range a little farther east, giant granite peaks that pricked the sky. On the other side of the river were the adobe hills, and rising above them were the cedar-covered ridges which held the Black Canyon of the Gunnison, a tremendous slash in the earth more than two thousand feet deep. To Mark it was the most awesome weight he had ever seen.

Mark rejoined the others, thinking that here was scenery which would never grow old to a man. He wished that Laura was standing beside him to see it, too. She would be here soon. Will Engles would not need more than a few days to throw up a log cabin that would do for a store, and then Laura would have kept her promise and she would be free to leave her father.

When he reached Ann and Draper, Mark said, "I thought this would be a good place for a dam. It would be easy to take a ditch out here. I think there's just about the right amount of fall to the land. I'll get my stakes down as soon as we eat." He nodded to Ann. "Then the rest of the mesa is yours."

She smiled. "Not quite. Just one hundred and sixty acres." She frowned. "But I don't have any idea how to figure how much that is or where to put the stakes."

"Nobody does, really," Mark said. "We're not surveyors. I'll pace it off, but that's just a little better than guessing. When this country is surveyed, we'll lose some land, but we'll gain some, too. I might lose my dam or part of my ditch or even my buildings, but it's a chance I've got to take."

"I guess it would be better if I took my claim down-stream from yours," Ann said. "That is, if you're going to let me use your ditch."

Mark nodded in agreement, reluctantly for he had not forgotten that Effie would in all probability be living with Ann. The thought of her using his ditch and being his neighbor still irritated him, and that was certainly what would happen now that she had taken part in the run. More than that, Ann was not capable of managing a ranch. If she stayed, Effie would have to come to her.

"I'll help you put your stakes down after I get mine in," he said. "There's another thing, Ann. You know you can't homestead on the reservation. You have to pre-empt the land. That is, you buy it for a dollar and a quarter an acre."

Ann turned away from him. "I guess I knew that, but I'd forgotten. I don't have any money, Mr. Manning. Not any at all."

She began to cry. Draper, who had been gathering wood along the creek for a fire, came to her and put an arm around her slender waist. "Don't cry, Miss Ann," he said. "You're getting a plum and Miss Effie is smart enough to see it even if she is bullheaded. She'll help you."

"Sure she will," Ann said, "and then I'll be beholden to her more than I am now."

"But there's a difference," Mark pointed out. "You're staking this claim. It would have to be a partnership."

Ann brightened. "Why, I hadn't thought of it that way. Of course it would, Mr. Manning."

Mark caught Draper's furtive wink as the preacher stooped to light the fire. Any man would help Ann, he thought, but it would take some doing to make Effie see the light. It would not be to her liking to take Ann or anyone else for a partner.

2

As soon as the noon meal was finished, Draper mounted one of the horses and, leading the other, said he'd better get back and bring the wagon. Effie would probably be there, and she'd be fuming and fawnching around, wondering where Ann was and why the horses were gone.

When Mark urged him to take either his rifle or revolver, Draper shook his head. "I'll be on my guard against Rawlins and Burris, but I don't think they will attack me. You're the one they'll try to kill and Ann's the one they want."

Draper stopped and tipped his head back to look at the sky, the hot sunshine falling on his bearded face. He said in what Mark judged to be half prayer and half confession, "I have never been one to hate my fellow men, but I hate Barney Burris and Dave Rawlins. Lord, forgive me and keep us safe from their ways of violence." Then he rode away.

"I guess you had better stay with me," Mark told Ann. "I can't look after you if you're a mile away. I've got a hunch that prayer of John's was for my benefit as well as the Lord's."

By evening the corners of Mark's and Ann's claims were located, white rags fluttering from the top of the stakes. Mark decided on his building site not far from where the dam would be, and pointed out a small ridge on Ann's claim, telling her it would be a good place for her cabin because water would not stand around it. That was something she had not thought of and she thanked him for the suggestion.

After supper he said, "We haven't seen hide nor hair of Rawlins and Burris all day, and that's worse than seeing them. They weren't trailing us this morning for the fun of it, so I figure they'll make their play tonight."

"You think they've been watching us?" she asked anxiously.

He nodded. "That's exactly what I think. I heard horses upstream a while ago, so I'm guessing they're hiding out in the willows along the creek till dark, then they'll try to pick us off. The minute you hear shooting, you get over under that bank and stay there till I tell you it's safe to come out. You may get your feet wet, but that's better than having them find you. It's a high bank and it's not likely you'll be found if you don't make any noise."

"Why haven't they done something before now?"

Mark shrugged. "Hard to tell. Maybe they're a little scared. They haven't had much luck with me and this time they don't want to take chances. And another thing. There'll be some claim jumping tonight. Maybe they figure on us thinking that's what they're doing. If they kill me but you don't see them, you couldn't swear who did it. Chances are the Army would just pass it off by saying they jumped my claim and decided afterward they didn't want it."

Ann shuddered, and asked in a low tone, "Mr. Manning, have I brought this trouble onto you by tagging along the way I have?"

"No," he told her quickly. "They've been wanting my hide from the day I first saw Laura Engle. Rawlins wants her and she favors me."

"But I am a burden," she said heavily. "You have to look out for me and I can't shoot a gun. And hit anything, I mean. I wish Effie was here. She's a good shot."

"Just you hike for that bank and you won't be a burden to me." He grinned as he filled his pipe. "If I have to choose between you and Effie, I'll take you every time."

She smiled tremulously. "Thank you, Mr. Manning. I was awfully mad at you when you wouldn't tell me where you were going to settle, but I shouldn't have been. Now that I've been with you all day, I realize what a kind man you are."

He pulled on his pipe and then shook his head, his thoughts on Will Engle. Mark could hate Dave Rawlins and Barney Burris with a clear conscious because they were the kind who deserved hatred, but Engle was a man of good intentions who would not knowingly or willfully harm anyone. Mark's feeling for Engle was one of contempt rather than hatred, and this, he told himself, was a sorry way to feel toward the man who was to be his father-in-law.

"No," he said after a time. "I'm not really a kind man."

"I think you are," she said firmly. She paused and asked hesitantly, "Are you going to marry Laura?" She flushed and glanced away. "I'm sorry. I have no right to ask a question like that."

"I'm not ashamed. Yes, I'm going to marry Laura as soon as her father gets a store going down on the river. I'll get a cabin up right away just on the chance we can get married in a few days.''

"Oh, I hope you can, Mr. Manning,'' Ann said breathlessly. ''I think it's wonderful. I envy Laura.'' She glanced away again. ''I just seem to keep saying the wrong thing all the time. I mean I envy Laura because she will have her home and a husband and babies.''

Mark rose and knocked his pipe against his boot heel, thinking he knew how Ann felt. She was a woman with empty arms who wanted babies more than anything else in the world. As he slipped his pipe into his pocket, he said, ''You're going to have to leave Effie. If you had a chance, you'd soon have your husband and home and babies, but I don't believe Effie will ever give you that chance.''

"Not if she can help it,'' Ann said bitterly, ''but Mr. Draper said I'd better stay with Effie this winter because it will be hard to get work in a new country like this. When spring comes . . .'' She stopped, staring at the fire. ''Mr. Manning, the trouble is I just don't know about things like that. I mean, I thought Dave Rawlins was a good man.''

"We have such men,'' Mark said. ''You'd be better off to live with Effie all your life than to marry a man like that.''

"I know that now,'' she said, ''but I didn't a few days ago.''

"You're tired. You'd better try to sleep because you may not sleep much later on.'' He carried his saddle and blanket to the bank of the creek and put them down. ''There's your bed. It'll get hard before morning, but it's the best this hotel has to offer.''

"It's your bed, Mr. Manning. I can't . . .''

"Yes you can. I'm not going to sleep if I can help it, but the way I feel now I'll have a hard time staying awake.''

"Then I'd better stay up and talk to you.''

He shook his head, knowing how tired she was. ''No, I'll sit up. It won't take much to wake me if I do drop off. I don't expect any trouble in the early part of the night. Rawlins will probably wait till just before dawn when he'll expect us to give up and go to sleep.''

He carried several armloads of dry wood from the creek

and dropped them beside the fire, then when the long twilight finally darkened into night, he moved back from the fire and sat down, his Winchester across his lap.

Ann fell asleep at once, he thought, for he could hear her steady breathing. Night sounds began coming to him: the cry of a bird that swept out of the darkness and was gone, the lonely call of a coyote from one of the rims to the west, the rustle of the willow leaves in the breeze, the steady, whispered conversation of the creek.

These were normal sounds, sounds that told him there was no danger yet. He lay back and stared at the coldly glittering stars and wondered about them as he had so often when he was working as a cowhand, then he felt sleep tugging at him and he sat up at once.

Still the excitement of the long day took its tribute, and in spite of all he could do, he began to nod until his chin rested on his chest and consciousness fled from him.

3

Mark's head jerked and stirred him awake. The fire had gone down. He rose and threw more wood on it, then quickly stepped back into the shadows, mindful of his suspicion that Barney Burris was the kind of man who would shoot an enemy from the cover of darkness if he had a chance.

Mark sat down again, his Winchester on the ground beside him. He was determined this time to remain awake, but a combination of silence, the fatigue and excitement of the day, and the droning lullaby of the creek was too much and once more he began to nod. A breaking twig followed by Ann's shrill scream of terror brought him to his feet and swept the cobwebs of sleep out of his head. He grabbed for his gun and had it half out of the holster when Burris called, "I've got the girl. You pull that iron and she gets a slug through the head."

He stood motionless for several seconds, cursing himself for dropping off to sleep the second time. He could barely make out the vague shape of the man between the fire and the willows. As well as he could see, Mark thought Burris was holding Ann in front of him.

"All right," Burris said. "That's better. Now toss your gun to the ground, slow and easy like and the girl will be safe enough. But you won't be, Manning. You're dead. I ain't a man to forget the pistol whipping you gave me in Central City."

"Or the beating you got the other day," Mark said.

Burris was silent, not wanting to be reminded of the fight. He had started it, never doubting his ability to hammer Mark into a bloody pulp, and his defeat must have been an enormous blow to his pride. Mark guessed that the memory of that whipping had festered in him until it was unbearable. That was why he had come alone, Mark thought, so that the satisfaction and the credit for killing the man who had beaten him would be entirely his.

Mark played the time out, hoping that his taunt would goad Burris into making some kind of mistake, but it didn't. Presently Burris asked, "You want to see the girl shot? Is that why you're waiting?"

Slowly Mark lifted the gun from leather and dropped it, thinking that it might be better for Ann if Burris killed her now. But there was always a chance against a slow-witted man like Burris, a chance Mark would not have felt he would have against Dave Rawlins.

"All right," Burris said. "You take your time doing it, but you finally do the smart thing. Now toss some wood on the fire. I want the girl to see how a man dies. Or are you a man, Manning? You were sleeping a hell of a long ways from the girl."

Mark stepped back to the fire and threw more wood on the coals, then moved back until he was within three feet of the dropped gun. A moment later the flames flared up and Mark had a clear view of Ann being held in front of Burris, a hairy arm hugging her breast. The other arm was at his side, a cocked gun in his hand, the barrel lined on Mark. Perhaps he'd never had any intentions of killing the girl, but it had been a potent threat to keep Mark from bolting into the darkness.

Now that the firelight gave Mark a chance to look at Ann, the faint hope that he had held flickered and died. If it had been Laura instead of Ann, there would have been a chance, but Ann was paralyzed by terror. She sagged like a sack of flour, all of her weight falling against Burris's arm, her head wobbling so that Mark thought she had fainted.

He waited through this long moment while death seemed only seconds away, his mind frantically searching for something, anything, which would give him a chance against Burris; the next moment Ann exploded. She suddenly and unexpectedly opened her mouth and bit the hand that was holding her, bringing an involuntary yell of pain from Burris. The next instant she slammed a heel down against his instep with all her strength, and began threshing around so that when he pulled the trigger, he missed by five feet.

Mark dived for his gun the instant Ann bit Burris's hand. He lay flat on the ground and tilted the barrel as Burris fired a second time and missed again. The big man's head and shoulders showed above the girl, but in the flickering firelight his bobbing head was a poor target. Burris failed to consider that. Apparently the only thought that occurred to him was that he couldn't shoot straight with the girl bouncing around as she was. He flung her away with so much force that she spun and fell ten feet from him.

Burris was swinging his gun into line when Mark shot him, the first bullet hitting him in the chest and knocking him back as violently as if an invisible rope had suddenly tightened and yanked him off his feet. As he started to fall, his head flung back. Mark squeezed off a second shot that caught him under the chin. He was dead when he sprawled out full length on the ground at the edge of the creek.

Mark rose and stood motionless for a moment, trembling, sweat pouring down his face. Then he holstered his gun and stepped away from the fire, wondering about Rawlins. Ann must be unconscious, he thought. She wasn't moving. Either the fall had knocked her out or she had fainted. Again she surprised him. Without moving, she called, "Mark, is he dead?"

He had considered her a helpless, clinging-vine type, and now he realized he had misjudged her. She was remaining motionless, knowing she was safer by doing so if Burris was still able to fight, and she was giving Mark a better chance by remaining out of the way.

"I think Burris is," Mark said, "but I don't know if Rawlins is somewhere around here or not. Stay where you are."

He edged around the fire, keeping away from the fringe of light. He reached Burris and felt for his pulse, but there was none. He dragged the body upstream so Ann would not see him, then he stood listening. Presently he heard the hammer of hoofs as someone rode away through the sagebrush.

Mark returned to the fire. "Rawlins just pulled out, Ann. I've got a hunch Burris was playing a solo game and Rawlins isn't a man to run any chances."

She rose and walked to him. Then she lost her self-control and began to tremble and cry. He tried to calm her and, failing, finally decided there was nothing to do but let her get over it herself in her own time. He led her to the blanket and saddle where she had been sleeping.

When he started to leave, she clung to him. "I'm afraid, Mark," she said. "Don't leave me. Please."

He lay down beside her. As if sure now that she was safe, she dropped off to sleep at once, an arm thrown across his chest. It was full of daylight when he woke. He discovered that her lips were almost touching his. When she saw that he was awake, she drew back and blushed.

"I'm sorry," she said, ashamed. "I didn't think you'd care if I kissed you when you were asleep. I was just thinking how much I owed you and how good you've been to me."

"I'll get the fire going," he said.

The wagon arrived near noon, Draper driving. This surprised Mark, for Effie sat beside him, apparently content to let the preacher handle the lines. When he stopped, she got down and ran to Ann, crying, "Did he lay a hand on you, honey? Did he touch you at all?"

Ann sighed. "You're such a fool, Effie. All men aren't monsters."

"Oh, you don't think so?" the big woman demanded. "Well, what about Dave Rawlins. You thought he was a fine man, now didn't you?"

"I was wrong about him," Ann said, "but Mr. Manning saved my life. He shot and killed Barney Burris."

"Well," Effie sniffed, "I'm glad you got Rawlins out of your head."

"If Burris is dead," Draper said, "then we can be sure of one thing. We haven't seen the last of Rawlins."

"If he shows up around here, I'll blow his head off," Effie said, unperturbed.

That afternoon Mark and Draper dug a grave for Burris, Effie giving them a canvas to wrap the body in. Draper read from the Bible and prayed and then they filled the grave, Draper saying, "I'm sorry, but I just can't help being thankful he's dead."

"So am I," Mark said. "That's nothing to be sorry about."

"It is with me," Draper said. "I feel I shouldn't be happy about the death of any of God's creatures, and we all are. Even Effie. You know, the soldiers caught her after dark and put her in the guardhouse with about fifty men they were holding. I guess no one knew she was a woman till it was daylight this morning and they released the prisoners. I judge it was a pretty rough experience for her, being locked up with all those men, and hating them the way she does. It gave her a little humility, which is something she hasn't had. I talked to her straight coming this morning, and for once she listened. She's going to let Ann think she's a partner and give her a little money now and then. It's not right, the way she's treated Ann."

"It sure isn't." Mark straightened and leaned on the shovel handle. "John, why don't you live with me this winter? I'd like to have company. You can work for me as much as you want and go out and preach whenever you feel like it."

"I take that offer kindly," Draper said, his gaze on Effie's wagon. "I don't know of any man I'd rather live with than you." He turned his head and studied Mark a moment, then he asked, "Are you telling me everything you've got in your head?"

"Well, maybe not." Mark grinned. "I figure Ann's going to need you and maybe you can do more with Effie than I can."

"Thank you. I'll be happy to make my home with you."

Mark shook his head. "It's my place to thank you," he said. "I will every time Effie comes around. I'll let you talk to her."

He spit on his hands and went back to work filling the grave, thinking what a paradox Ann was, then his mind turned to Laura and he wondered how soon she would free herself to marry him.

Part 3

The Settlement

10

Mark Manning

1

The sun was well up on this day in May 1882 when the smell of coffee and bacon woke Mark. John Draper called from where he stood by the stove, "If you're going to swim this morning, Mark, get it done. You've got about five minutes."

Mark rose and drew on his pants. "Give me ten," he said, and ran out of the cabin to the pond backed up by the dam he and Draper had built during the winter. He took off his pants and made a long, clean dive from the bank, the water shocking him and driving the last cobweb of sleep from his head.

He swam upstream to where the water was shallow, then swam back to the dam again. The water was cold, but it did not seem so after he had survived the first shock. Although it was still May, the weather had been hot for nearly a week during the days, with the nights still sharp. He crawled out of the water and ran his hands down over his long, hard-muscled body, then he pulled his pants on.

The fall and winter had been fruitful in many ways, he thought. John Draper had lived with him and helped him except during the days when he was preaching to the settlers in the valley. Age had not slowed Draper. He was a good worker and a fine craftsman with tools and wood, and Mark had said once, "I don't believe you're a blacksmith. I think you're a carpenter. Maybe a cabinet maker."

Draper had smiled and said, "I have been at times. But I'm also a blacksmith. As a matter of fact, there are a number of things I can do passing well, but you'll remember that St. Paul was a tentmaker. Still, preaching the word was the most important thing in the world to him. It is to me, too."

Now Mark looked around with pride at the dam, the
tight little cabin, the log shed, the corral, the patch of
ground that was cleared of sagebrush. He walked slowly
back to the cabin, knowing that Draper would be impatient
if he didn't return before the breakfast was spoiled. A
fruitful winter, he told himself again. Fortunately the weather
had been mild so that they had not been kept indoors very
often. With Draper's help, he had accomplished far more
than he'd expected last September.

Still, he wasn't satisfied with himself or his life. He
should be, he thought. Dave Rawlins had not bothered
him. Ann and Effie had proved to be the best of neighbors,
and this had been as big a surprise to Draper as it was to
Mark.

Probably the main reason for his dissatisfaction was his
failure to marry Laura. He loved her more than ever, and
he was as sure of her love as man could be sure of any
other human's emotion. But the problem remained the
same. Almost nine months had passed since the run and
nothing had changed.

Will Engle's store was a failure. He still needed Laura,
so for one reason or another the wedding had been post-
poned for a day, a week, a month, and now, although
Mark understood how Laura felt, he was plagued by the
chilling fear that the problem never would change and
therefore Laura would never be his wife.

She came to see him every Sunday when the weather
was fit. Perhaps she was glad to get away from her father
and the empty store and the smothering frustrations from
which there was no escape as long as she remained there.
Still, she would not set a date, and Mark had almost
reached the point of giving her an ultimatum.

He entered the cabin and drew on his shirt and buttoned
it; he opened his pants and shoved his shirttail into them
then buttoned them and pulled his belt tight. He ran a
comb through his wet hair and sat down at the table.
Draper had made all the furniture, borrowing tools from
Effie and working inside the cabin during the long winter
evenings and the snowy days when there was little that
could be done outside.

Draper sat down across from Mark and asked the blessing, then Mark reached for the coffeepot and filled his cup. He asked, "Preaching in Montrose today?"

Draper nodded. "I think we'll be able to put up a building before fall."

Montrose was the nearest town, a settlement of log cabins on the other side of the river. Mark seldom went there because he felt obligated to buy his and Draper's supplies at Will Engle's store, although he despised Engle so much that he could hardly stand the man long enough to be waited on. Laura apparently sensed this. At least she never asked Mark to visit her in her cabin, but had always been willing to saddle Fox and ride to the top of the mesa.

Mark helped himself to the bacon and flapjacks, and said, "I hope you do get a building, John." He poured a liberal covering of syrup over the flapjacks and added, "I suppose you'll be leaving me when that happens. You'll have to live in town, won't you?"

"I suppose so," Draper said absently, then glanced at Mark. "Is Lieutenant Mills coming to see Ann again today?"

Mark nodded. "He planned to when he stopped here last Sunday."

"Is he going to marry her?"

"I wouldn't be surprised. He's been a steady visitor most of the winter." Mark laughed. "You've got to admit, John, that a man has to have a mighty important reason to stand up against Effie the way he has."

"She hasn't encouraged him for a fact," Draper admitted. "Once I chided Mills about waiting so long to declare himself. The lieutenant had said sharply, 'Effie's improved this winter. Maybe if I wait long neough, she'll improve some more.' He paused, then he added bitterly, 'I never thought I was a coward, but I'm scared of that woman. I heard what she did to Dave Rawlins. What could you do if a woman like that starts beating you?'

"I thought a while," Draper said, "and then I told him that I'd try to answer such questions in terms of my understanding of Christ's teachings, but that I know nothing in the Gospel that bears on such a situation. However, I am convinced that Jesus would say if a woman wanted to live like a man, then let her do so. I would hit her back, Lieutenant!"

Mark thought about this conversation and reflected that Draper would do exactly as he had advised Mills to do. Perhaps Effie knew that, for she had treated Draper with more respect than she did most men.

Draper finished his breakfast and pushed his plate back. He said, "Mark, I guess you know by this time that my conscience is often a red-hot fire inside me. That's why I must talk to you about the condition of your soul. You have told me you have never been baptized. I have known few men whose morals and integrity I respect more than yours. That is the reason I have put off talking to you. This morning I realized I could not put it off any longer for the reason you just mentioned. I will have to leave here sometime this summer."

Mark reached for the coffeepot and filled his cup again. He had respected Draper because the preacher had not tried to convert him, but now the old man was leaning forward, his eyes burning with a zealot's fire.

"Let it ride, John," Mark murmured. "I made my decision a long time ago."

"No, I have to say this," Draper said doggedly. "Baptism and confession are the doors to Heaven. I know how you feel, Mark. There is nothing in your belief about God or man to keep you from being baptized and confessing the name of Jesus. It would be a great tragedy if you were condemned to eternal punishment because of this neglect. The pond is handy, Mark. Effie and Ann could be witnesses. Don't put it off."

"You believe your way, John," Mark said, "and I'll believe mine. If I saw God as you do, I could not worship Him."

Draper spread a big hand and waved it forbiddingly in front of his face. "Don't say that, Mark. Don't say it. It's blasphemy. I'm only trying to do my duty."

"I know, John," Mark said. "Now let me ask you an important question. You know how I feel about the Utes. There are good ones and bad ones just the same as there are good and bad whites. I have never injured the Utes, but my government has. It has broken its word. It has used the military force of a strong nation to make a handful of people do what it says. This is not justice, John. The Utes are people and have the same human rights we do, the rights that great men like Thomas Paine and Thomas Jefferson once wrote about.''

The preacher shrugged his thick shoulders. ''What's done is done. You and I cannot change it. We couldn't have changed the course of events even when the Indians were here. It's the story of all mankind from the beginning of history.''

Draper had said this before, but to Mark it still did not answer anything. He said, ''I knew Ouray personally, John. He was a great and honest man in his way. He once said, 'Our home is here. On the prairie the Ute is like a wolf in a trap. Here he is like an eagle among the peaks. There is room for all. Let the white people have the prairies and give us the mountains. We are happy among the mountains and the white people do not need them.'

''Well, it's true. We were wrong when we took this land from them. That's why I'm asking you this question, John. Am I compounding a felony by taking a claim on the reservation? Is this God you know so well going to punish me because I'm doing something which I know in my heart is wrong?''

''Of course not. In a few years you'll have a fine ranch where the Indians would have only pitched a tepee or hunted deer or fished in the creek. You'll be raising beef to feed hungry people. If you don't take the land, someone else will, so what you do isn't important either way.'' He rose. ''I'd better go, Mark, if you'll take care of the dishes. I have to see some people this morning before the service starts.''

''I'll do the dishes,'' Mark said. ''Go ahead.''

He stood in the doorway while Draper put on his coat and hat and walked to the corral where he saddled Mark's horse. Watching him, Mark wondered how any man who felt he had been called to preach the Gospel could be as completely wrong as John Draper.

2

Draper had ridden off on Mark's horse and the dishes were finished when Mark glanced through the north win-

dow and saw Effie approaching in her leggy, manlike
stride. He always laughed when he saw her walk in that
purposeful manner, her big rump flopping behind her. She
was thoroughly confused, he thought. She claimed to hate
men and yet she tried to live like a man. In any case, she
could not disguise the obvious fact that she was a woman.

If he had seen Effie approaching this way a few months
ago, he would have fled and left Draper to do the talking if
the preacher was home, but now he felt as Lieutentant
Mills did, that Effie had improved. Perhaps mellowed
was a better word. He had even made an arrangement to
swap his and Draper's labor for the use of her team.
Whenever they had worked together as when they had
built her cabin, Effie had held up her end, insisting that
she wasn't going to be outdone by any man.

Mark put the coffeepot back on the front of the stove
and stood in the doorway waiting for her, the warm morning sun falling upon him. He watched Effie, smiling as he
speculated on what had changed her. She had gone along
with the fiction that the ranch would be a partnership with
Ann and whatever profit was made would be divided
between the two of them.

During the fall Effie had talked to enough people who
had settled on the other side of the river and had observed
their effort to work the ground so that she realized the land
Ann had claimed was better than most of the valley. She
had seen some of the settlers' chickens pick up the adobe
soil after a rain until it formed great balls on their feet that
had to be removed by hand. She had seen men try to plow
the land when it was dry and hard; she had watched them
attempt to work it when it was too wet, and finally in a
moment of weakness she had thrown up her hands and
said, "I'd move back to the Arkansas in a week if I had
that kind of ground."

"That was where you wanted to settle," Ann reminded
her.

Effie had nothing to say to that. She once admitted to
Mark that she was surprised at what Ann had done in
following Mark the morning of the run, and she even
grudgingly admitted that Ann had shown both courage and
wisdom. Effie was not a person to make mistakes, but,

having made one, it was Mark's opinion she wasn't likely to admit it. This time she did, perhaps for the first time in her life, and it was that, Mark thought, which had mellowed her more than anything else.

When Effie reached the cabin, he said, "Good morning, neighbor. I saw you coming and I put the coffeepot back on the stove."

He stepped out of the doorway. She came in and dropped into a chair at the table, puffing a little. "Thank you kindly," she said. "I can stand a cup of coffee." She took a long breath. "I guess I'm getting fat."

"You need to work harder, Effie," he said.

She bridled at once. "What the hell are you talking about? I work hard."

Mark laughed. "Sure you do. You just never know when you're being joshed."

She started to say something, checked herself, and then demanded, "That coffee hot yet?"

"I think so," he said, and poured a cup for her.

"The grass is up," she said. "Or will be by the time we get any cows on it. When are we going to Gunnison to buy our cattle?"

They had talked about this before, agreeing that it was important to get their cattle on the mesa before it was settled. They couldn't hold the mesa indefinitely, of course, but they probably could until the river and bigger creek valleys were settled. After that the new settlers would take up the mesa land. By that time they hoped to have a big enough herd to make it worthwhile to hire several cowhands and keep the cattle among the aspens on the divide during the summer.

"I don't know," Mark said. "I guess we'd better go next month."

"Well, I think so," she said as if he were to blame for the fact they hadn't gone already. She took a drink of coffee and put the cup down. "That wasn't what I came over for, although I told Ann it was. I hate like hell to ask a man for advice, but I guess you're the best there is. What sort of yahoo is this here Lieutentant Mills who keeps coming around?"

"He's got guts or he wouldn't buck you," Mark said, "and I think he's in love with Ann."

"Yeah, yeah," Effie grunted, "and she's got so many stars in her eyes over him she can't live from one Sunday to the next." She glared at Mark. "You know I don't trust men. All they think of is . . ."

"Yes, Effie," he said. "I know exactly what you think all men want, but you're wrong. I mean, some men are as decent as you are. As far as Ann's concerned, she's wanted a family as long as I've known her."

"I know it," Effie snapped, "though I don't know why. Sure, some men are kind o' decent. Draper is because he's so old he can't be no other way, and you're decent 'cause you're in love with Laura Engle and you don't want nothing to happen that'd make her mad."

She chewed her lower lip a moment, then she said, "There was one funny thing about you. Ann told me that on the night you shot Barney Burris she got purty scared, kind o' hysterical, and you comforted her and held her in your arms while she slept. She woke up when it was daylight and she kissed you 'cause you'd been good to her. It makes me wonder about you, just the two of you and that simple-minded Ann trusting any man who was kind to her."

He walked to the door and stood looking out across the mesa to the crest of the divide. He remained silent until his anger cooled. At times like this Effie irritated him to the place where it was all he could do to keep from treating her like the man she seemed to want to be. It would be senseless to tell her that some men were decent enough not to take advantage of a girl as naïve as Ann. She just wouldn't believe it.

Finally he turned to Effie. "I was figuring to marry Laura in a week. Let's let it go at that."

"Sure," Effie said. "I'm sorry it hasn't worked out. Laura's a good girl and that there father of her'n . . ." She stopped, shrugged her thick shoulders, and added, "Well, I done my best to take care of Ann ever since she came to live with me. I've run men off by the dozen, but I can't go on doing it, seems like. That's why I want to know about

Mills. If he's like most men, I'll shoot his head off the next time he shows up.''

"He's not," Mark said. "Not what you're thinking most men are. Effie, if you're asking for plain talk, I'll give it to you. I guess you see yourself as a mother. That's all right. Ann's needed somebody like you, but now she wants a husband and a home. She won't be happy till she's a wife and mother, and if you go on keeping her from being what she wants to be, she'll hate you and wind up leaving you."

Effie glared at him. "My God, Manning, you're like all men. You think you know everything. To hell with you. I don't know why I . . . I . . .''

She stopped, choking, as the tears suddenly began rolling down her seamed, weather-beaten face. She rubbed her sleeve across her eyes and tried to say something, but her lips were quivering so much she couldn't speak. It was the first sign of weakness he had ever seen in her, and he knew that he had said what needed to be said, a truth she had realized, but had refused to admit to herself.

"Effie," Mark said, "let her marry Mills. They'll have some problems they'll have to work out. All Army couples do, but let her try."

She wiped her eyes with her sleeve again. "I don't know why I'm blubbering like any woman. I ain't just any woman."

"Now there's a point I'll agree with you one hundred per cent," he said.

"You don't know how it's been, Manning," she said. "I never loved anybody in my life. I guess I never even knew what love was, but she was so damned helpless when I found her in Pueblo and she needed me. Well, I took her in and I got so I loved her and I think she loves me. I took care of her and I looked after her and now she wants to get married and leave me. I'll be just as lonesome as I used to be."

"She still loves you, Effie," Mark said, "and she always will if you let her go, but if you keep her from getting married, I tell you she'll end up hating you."

Effie glared at him a moment, then she rose and stomped out of the cabin and strode back to her place. Watching

her, Mark thought she had been right in saying he didn't
know how it had been. Ann's coming into her life was
probably the best thing that had ever happened to her, and
it was natural for her to want to keep the girl, but now he
thought she could give Ann up.

11

Laura Engle

1

When Laura woke Sunday morning, her first thought was
of Mark. She kept thinking of him as she built a fire and
cooked breakfast for herself and her father, and while she
did the dishes after Will Engle left her cabin and returned
to the store. She had spent every Sunday with Mark since
the run except one in March which had been so stormy she
couldn't see across the river.

The hours she spent with Mark went too fast and were
too few. When she got back Sunday evening, she started
looking forward to the next Sunday morning when she
would see him again. The time she spent with him was all
that had kept her going through the fall and winter and
spring, the longest nine months of her life.

Now that Sunday morning was here again, she could
hardly wait to finish the dishes and put on her riding skirt
and blouse. She ran out of the cabin to the corral and
saddled Fox, thinking how her father had objected to her
buying him in Gunnison last summer. Will Engle had been
wrong as he was wrong about most things. If she had not
bought the gelding, she would not have seen Mark so often
as she did, she couldn't even have escaped from this place
with its frustration and sense of defeat.

She mounted, thinking that at least her father had built a
cabin for her so she had not been forced to spend the
winter in a tent. The first cabin he had built was the store.
He slept in the back and spent little time in her cabin

except to eat, and so, since she was not in the store very much, she actually did not see a great deal of him. That suited her because she did not enjoy his company.

She waved to him as she rode past the front of the store. He was sitting in the sunshine on a bench he had hewed from a cottonwood log. He half-lifted a limp hand to her as she went by, saying nothing and not even giving her a hint of a smile. She thought angrily that he was jealous of the few hours of happiness she was able to squeeze out of the week.

The store was a complete failure, but Whit Bailey, who had the claim closest to the Army post, was highly successful. Laura's father had staked off some town lots and put up a sign announcing that this was Engle City, but no one had bought any lots or even shown any interest in buying any. Other men had done the very thing Mark had suggested last summer. They had started a town which they had named Montrose near where Cedar Creek came down to the Uncompahgre, and they were selling lots "hand over fist" as Will Engle put it after returning from the new town.

Laura followed the road along the river for a time, then angled across the bottom that was covered by chico brush and climbed to the mesa, her thoughts on her father. He didn't attempt to continue the illusion of starting a town and running a store. They had eaten most of the supplies that had filled the shelves last September. Oh, he had sold a few things to Mark, and on one occasion Effie Allen had bought some groceries. Once in a while a traveler driving to the Army post or Ouray had stopped, but the roadside business had not amounted to much.

Eventually her father had sold both teams and wagons without asking Laura or even telling her. Now that money was spent, too. The last time he had gone to Montrose he had gambled and got drunk, and had spent the night alongside the road between his store and Montrose. When he staggered into Laura's cabin the next day, he was sick and filthy. She had turned him around and given him a push toward the river, saying, "I don't want to see you till you're cleaned up."

Now there was only enough food left on the shelves for

about two more weeks. She still had her five hundred dollars and he would expect her to use it to keep them eating. She wouldn't do it, she told herself. As long as she pampered him, he would go on the way he had. So, once more, she promised herself she would tell Mark she would marry him in a week or any day he set.

Will Engle was a beaten man. This was something she could not understand. As far back as she could remember, he had always put up the big front, talked about the big dream, the pot of gold which was at the end of the rainbow just over the next hill. Now the big front, the self-deceit, the big I were all gone. He knew she felt only contempt for him, she thought. He had wasted her money, he had lost his chance, and now he sat wallowing in self-pity. He would probably end up being a saloon bum. She didn't want to be around if he did.

She saw Mark's cabin ahead of her and put Fox into a gallop. John Draper would be gone by now, and Ann and Effie never came around when she was there. They probably gossiped about her and thought the worst of her and Mark, but she didn't care. Nothing really mattered any more except the precious hours each week that she had with Mark.

He was waiting for her. When she stopped, he held up his arms and she fell into them and hugged and kissed him, shutting her eyes and holding to him as if for a little while she had wiped out all the rest of the world and its problems and its frustrations, and there was just her and Mark. But when she opened her eyes, the rest of the world was still there just as it had been before she closed them.

She drew her head back and sighed. "Oh, Mark, I have no shame. I love you so much."

"Is it good to be ashamed if you love a man?" he asked.

She laughed. "Of course not, but a woman should never be bold or aggressive."

He took the reins and led Fox toward the corral, Laura walking beside him, her hand on his arm. He said thoughtfully, "I don't know about that. I think I like for my woman to be just a little aggressive."

"Like Effie?"

He shook her head, grinning. "I said a *little* aggressive."

He off-saddled and turned Fox into the corral, then walked to the pond, Laura still holding to his arm. They sprawled in the grass, Mark motioning to the pond. "Let's go swimming. I went in before breakfast and it was cold then, but it's warmer now. You'd like it."

"I don't have a suit and you know it."

"You could swim without a suit."

"Mark, I'm surprised at you."

"You said you had no shame."

She laughed. "Well, it's just that your female neighbors might see me."

He told her about Effie coming over early that morning. Laura said, "I hope it works out between her and the lieutenant." Then she sat up and, hugging her knees, dropped her chin upon them. "Mark, Ann isn't the only one with a feeling of empty arms. I'm not going on this way the rest of my life. I know I've said it before, but this time I'll do it. Tell your preacher friend he can marry us next week. Then we'll go after the cattle like Effie wants to. I'll give you my money so you can buy a bigger herd."

He sat up and looked at her questioningly. "You really mean it this time?"

"I never meant anything more in my life, Mark. I know I've shilly-shallied back and forth and I wouldn't blame you if you started looking for another girl. This could go on all my life. I'm not going to let it."

"I guess that's about the best news I ever heard," he said, and reached for her.

When he let her go, she brushed her hair back, whispering breathlessly, "You don't know what you do to me, Mark." She lay in his arms, the warm sun beating down upon her, and she was quite content.

2

Laura left late in the afternoon, at peace with herself for the first time in months. She had never told Mark the whole story about her father and why she had stayed with him through the winter. She thought about it now as she rode, the sun far down in the west, her long shadow moving across the sagebrush beside her.

Last September, Will Engle and Charley McGivern built the store cabin and put up the shelves, then moved the supplies from the wagon into the building, filling the shelves and piling the heavier sacks and barrels on the floor until there was hardly room to move along the aisle. Engle kept one counter near the door empty, for this was where he intended to set a keg of whisky. He had forgotten where the whisky was in the loaded wagons, and they were nearly empty before he discovered it was gone.

At first he couldn't believe it and began hunting through the supplies that were in the store, thinking they had carried the whisky in and then forgotten it. Then he went through the boxes that were still in the wagons, but there simply wasn't any whisky. He returned to the store and looked around. He hadn't seen it since it had been loaded in Gunnison. As far as he knew, no one had tampered with the freight. The wagons had never been left unguarded. He couldn't understand it, and Laura, watching him, sensed that he still didn't believe it was gone.

"Laura, you know anything about it?" he demanded.

"No," she answered. "Why would I?"

"I dunno," he muttered, "but it sure is the damnedest thing I ever seen. Charley, you know anything about it?"

"No," McGivern said, swallowing.

It had to be him, Laura told herself. She had never trusted or liked the man, and now, staring at him, she saw a flush crawl across his face as he began backing away. She said, "Pa, take a good look at Charley. He knows."

McGivern started to run. Engle caught up with him and gripped him by the nape of the neck and shook him. The old man had no fight in him. He bleated in terror like a hurt sheep, and then the words tumbled out of him, how that Barney Burris and Dave Rawlins had held him up one Sunday morning while almost everyone else along the Gunnison was attending church service. They took the whisky and helped him replace the other supplies in the wagon so Engle wouldn't know the load had been tampered with and told McGivern they'd cut his throat if he ever mentioned it to anyone. From what they said, they planned to smuggle the whisky onto the reservation and sell it to Colorow.

Laura had never seen her father lose his temper. Not as completely as he did then. He went berserk, choking McGivern and beating his head against the ground. He would have killed the old man if Laura hadn't picked up a club and hit him. McGivern crawled off and got to his feet and started down the road.

Neither Laura nor her father ever saw Charley McGivern after that. If he had stayed, Engle would have forgiven him. He needed the old man to talk to, to be big to, to laugh at his jokes, but now McGivern was gone, and Laura wondered if the old man had taken part of her father with him, the big front behind which he had found a sort of security. Or was it because the whisky was gone, the one commodity which he had been certain he could sell at a very large profit.

Laura wasn't sure of anything except that her father had cried that night, cried like an unhappy child who could not face the future. He quit making big promises, he didn't talk any more about the big dream, the one more opportunity which had somehow slipped out of his fingers without any fault on his part. He told her she was like her mother; she had strength and faith and courage, and she must not leave him because he could not live without her. He would kill himself if she did.

So she stayed, somehow finding a little pity along with the contempt for his abject cowardice. Since then she had not said anything about marrying Mark, but she would tonight. Perhaps he would break down again and beg her to stay, but she would not. She either had to marry Mark or break off with him, and she could not do that. Somehow she had to make her father understand she would not carry him on her back the rest of her life.

When she reached the road, she saw John Draper coming from Montrose. She stopped, deciding to burn her bridges behind her. She said, "Good evening, Mr. Draper."

He reined up and tipped his hat to her. He said, "May the Lord show you His shining face, Miss Laura. Did you and Mark have a pleasant day?"

"Very pleasant," she said. "Mark tells me you will be

leaving his place soon and that you plan to put up a church in Montrose."

He nodded. "The plans are now definite. We worked hard on it today. We have pledges for both work and money which will be sufficient to erect a building."

"I'm glad," she said. "You see, I'm about to move in with you and I guess that would make the cabin a little crowded."

He laughed. "I'm afraid it would. I'm glad to hear it, Miss Laura. What is the date?"

"We haven't set the day," she said. "I'll talk to my father tonight, but Mark and I thought in about a week. Mark will talk to you. Of course we want you to marry us."

"Good," he said. "I would be most happy to do so." He hesitated, then he said, "Miss Laura, will you be happy, living here on the reservation?"

She stared across the river at the adobe hills. They were the same color in spring they were at any other time of the year. Almost nothing grew on them, and sometimes when she stared at the mounds and gullies that had been formed by countless centuries of erosion, she had the terrifying sensation that they were the paws of some lurking monster that were reaching for her and would seize her and the monster would swallow her. She shuddered and turned her face so she could not see them, thinking she had never had a more ridiculous feeling in her life.

"I hate this country," she said, "but I'll live here if Mark wants to."

"Mark doesn't, but I don't think he knows it yet," Draper said. "It's all foolishness, of course, but he knew Ouray and some of the other Utes when he worked at the Agency, and so he has a guilty feeling about taking part of their land. He's like Jacob who wrestled with God all one night after he sent his family across the ford of the Jabbok. Mark will wrestle with God as long as he's here."

"But you've both worked so hard," she protested. "It's crazy, just to walk off and leave everything."

"Of course it's crazy," Draper agreed, "but it would be crazier to live here five years and have this thing grow on him until he had to leave it then. I just thought it was something you ought to talk over."

He touched the brim of his hat and rode through the chico brush to the mesa. She turned Fox upstream toward the store, her thoughts fixed so firmly on what Draper had said that she did not see Dave Rawlins until he rose from where he had been sitting on the river bank.

He stepped into the road and tipped his hat, saying, "Good evening, Laura. Your father said you were on the mesa, so I've been waiting to talk to you."

She reined up, staring at him and uncertain about what to do. She had not seen much of him since the run, although he had ridden along the road many times. He was as handsome, immaculate, and gentle-mannered as ever, and still she was instinctively afraid of him just as she had been when Barney Burris was alive.

"Get out of my way," she said. "I don't want to talk to you."

"I think you will." He gripped one of the reins, his head tipped back. "I have something to tell you which is of great importance to your father. He's lost now, Laura. He needs success. I can give it to him."

"Well?"

"I'm working on something that's big," he said, "something that can make a fortune for a lot of us. That includes your father. Whether it does is up to you. Let me add one more thing. This country will develop in the years ahead. A railroad's coming. More people will settle here. The San Juan mines are just beginning to produce. I'm not bragging unduly when I say I will grow with the country."

"Good luck to you," she said. "Now if you'll let me go . . ."

"Wait," he said. "I don't want to grow old alone. I love you, Laura. I've never had a chance to tell you before because you would never let me, but I'm telling you now. Will you marry me?"

She stared at him, finding it impossible to believe he had said what she had heard. But he stood in front of her, tall and straight and serious-faced, waiting for her answer.

"No," she said. "Now will you let me go?"

"You will," he said in a tone of certainty. "I think you will decide in my favor within a week. Next Sunday we're having a meeting in your father's grove."

He stepped away and she rode on, frightened by what sounded as if it were a note of destiny in his voice. She didn't know anything about a meeting or the big something Rawlins was working on or how it involved her father. He wouldn't be likely to tell her if she asked. She didn't have to tell him about her and Mark. Not yet anyhow. They were going to wait a week, so there was no hurry.

Why had Rawlins been so certain she would marry him when she had never done anything to encourage him? She had no answer, but still it frightened her, and she wondered if he held some string of destiny of which she was not aware.

12

Dave Rawlins

1

Dave Rawlins stood in the road watching Laura ride away; he felt his pulse pounding in his temples and was immediately annoyed with himself. He did not know why he reacted to Laura Engle the way he did. He wanted her more than he'd ever wanted any woman in his life, wanted her so much that it had become a mania with him, a compulsion so strong that he was even willing to make her big wind of a father part of his plan.

When he could not see Laura any longer, he returned to the river bank and sat down and smoked a cigarette, thinking about her. The simplest explantion was that Laura did not want him, therefore she presented a challenge and made the game of pursuit an exciting one. Another might be that right from the first she had preferred Mark Manning to him, and that made less sense because Manning was the kind who would never have anything better to offer Laura than hard work on a ranch, and she deserved a better life than that.

Such simple explanations did not quite answer his ques-

tion. Perhaps it was a combination of them along with Laura's
good looks and her tall, leggy figure and her quiet dignity,
plus his conviction that she would be the kind of wife who
would fit into his plans for the future. Whether he wanted her
because of his plans, or whether he had made his plans because of her was a question in his mind, but one thing was
sure. He had matured since Barney Burris had been shot by
Mark Manning, and now he had an aim in life.

He rose and tossed his cigarette into the river that was
high and muddy this time of year with the spring runoff.
He had not grieved over Burris's death. As a matter of
fact, he had been glad. If it hadn't happened, they would
soon have parted company. Once Rawlins had begun to
see the opportunities that presented themselves to men
with vision and a glib tongue, he realized that the old
poker-playing, woman-chasing, drifting kind of life he
had led with Burris was a thing of the past. Here he
needed to be respectable, and Barney Burris and respectability had always been complete strangers.

Rawlins would take care of Mark Manning. That was as
certain in his mind as it was that spring followed winter or
the sun would come up in the morning, but it would be in
his own time and way, and not because he had killed
Burris who had been a fool. Burris and he had planned the
first attack carefully, agreeing to wait until nearly dawn
when Manning would probably be sound asleep. They
were going to come at him from both sides so that if he got
the drop on one of them, the other would still get him, but
Burris wouldn't wait. He must have sat there beside the fire
brooding about the beating Manning had given him, letting
it fester in him until he felt he had to settle the debt himself.

No, Rawlins wouldn't revenge Burris's death, but as
long as Manning was around, he stood between Laura and
Rawlins, so he had to go, but Rawlins was patient. He
could wait until the right opportunity presented itself.

Rawlins mounted and rode downstream to Montrose,
remembering how the big idea had come to him last fall
shortly after the run. He saw a farmer trying to repair a
break in a ditch he had from the river, but the man had
turned too much water into the ditch and it had torn out
one side and had made a quagmire all around his cabin.

Foolish, Rawlins thought, for fifty settlers to dig fifty ditches. The expense and labor would be great, and more than that, none of the ditches would be built right. They would be constantly breaking, with the water being wasted and in many cases doing harm to the fields. What the valley needed was a large irrigation project, a ditch company with sufficient capital to build canals big enough to do the job, and if the settlers pooled their resources, and reached out to take in other investors such as bankers, the thing could be done. Dave Rawlins was the man to promote it.

From that day on Dave Rawlins donned the cloak of respectability. He dressed well. He was careful to avoid any overt act that would make anyone think he was not a pillar of community life. He even attended the services of several religious groups which had been organized in the valley, and this included John Draper's.

If he visited a brothel in Ouray, he did so late at night, and if he happened to meet a brother community pillar, it was tacitly understood that neither would advertise the meeting. If he played poker in Ouray, it was only with the bankers, the mine operators, or the newly arrived Easterners who were looking for an investment. If he stepped into a saloon for a drink, it was one of the best catering to the carriage trade.

It was a new and heady life for him and he wondered why he had spent so much time drifting around with men like Barney Burris who lived one small notch above the animal level. Out here in a new country like this he needed no pedigree; people took him for what he said he was, a man from Oregon looking for an opportunity to invest his money and develop the country at the same time.

He found he could speak the farmer's language and he spent most of his time with them, riding up and down the valley and talking about its bright future as he visited with them. They considered him one of them and not a visiting city slicker, probably because he often spent a day grubbing sagebrush with them or helping build a shed or giving a hand castrating a litter of pigs or anything else that needed to be done. He soiled many a white shirt and he always carried an extra pair of pants rolled up and tied behind his saddle, but it was worth the trouble because he had hit upon the one sure way to secure acceptance.

He was very circumspect in his relationship to the women, although he was quite aware of the sighing among the farmers' daughters all up and down the valley and the inviting glances they gave him. He took pride in the knowledge that he could, if he wanted to, have some of the wives as well, but he resisted the temptation, fully aware that almost anything would be overlooked except that. The fact that he had been a hard drinker and poker player in Gunnison the summer before was a case in point. It was forgotten or overlooked by men who had known him then, as was also the fact that he had been a close friend of Barney Burris the brawler.

Reaching Montrose, he put his horse in the livery stable, thinking that in time there would be a city here instead of a collection of adobe huts and log cabins, many of which gave the strange impression of having grown there, for some of the logs had thrown out live branches since the cabins had been built.

He ate supper in a restaurant and then dropped into a saloon for a drink. There he met a banker and one of the town fathers. He asked casually, "You'll be at the meeting at Engle's grove next Sunday, won't you? We need solid citizens like you men."

The banker, Luke Mack, slapped him on the back and laughed. "And you need solid gold from us solid citizens, don't you, Dave?"

"Of course we do," Rawlins said frankly. "You don't build a ditch system without money, and you don't develop a country like this without water being put on the land. What do we get here, about nine inches of precipitation a year?"

Abner Day, the town father, nodded. "Something like that. He's right, Luke. Water is the lifeblood of this kind of country. I've sunk most of my money into developing this town site, but one thing's sure. If the farmers around here don't make it, Montrose won't, either."

"Got any of your wad left to buy water company stock?" Mack asked.

"A little," Day said. "And what I have left is going there, too." He motioned toward Rawlins. "It strikes me that Dave here is the kind of man we need, a man with vision and a willingness to gamble his own money."

"I agree to that." Mack slapped Rawlins on the back again. "Yes sir, I agree to that, and the bank will back you." He laughed. "Let's say, up to ten thousand dollars. You're organizing Sunday?"

"That's right," Rawlins said. "I had a map made of the proposed project and I'll have it on exhibit. First we'll take pledges, and then I'll report on an estimate I have of the cost of the work. After that we'll organize and sell stock if anybody has the money. We should be able to start actual work in a few days."

"I hear you're bringing a band up from Ouray to add to the festivities," Day said.

"That's right," Rawlins said. "I'm also furnishing beer for the men and lemonade for the women and children. We're asking the women to bring picnic baskets."

"It will be quite an occasion," the banker said. "I wouldn't miss it."

Rawlins excused himself and went to his room in the hotel. He sat up long enough to smoke a cigarette, thinking about Laura and wondering if her father could actually influence her. Will Engle was a big blow. Hardly even a breeze now, with the way things had gone this winter, but he'd do all he could with Laura. Rawlins was sure of that if he dangled a little money in front of Engle's nose, maybe one thousand dollars.

All that Rawlins wanted was a chance to talk to the girl, to take her buggy riding and perhaps dancing. He had never met a woman who could resist his charm if he had a chance to court her. The trouble was Laura had never given him a chance. Engle could persuade her to at least do that, he thought.

He took off his clothes and blew out the lamp, then lay down on the bed. It was warm evening, the room holding the day's heat so that he was comfortable lying there completely naked. He had done very well with his assets, he thought, remembering what the town father had said to the banker. "Dave is the kind of man we need, a man with vision and a willingness to gamble his own money."

Sure, he'd gamble all he had, about ten thousand dollars, but that would be a small amount to what he'd take out of the company once he had it going. The money, he

knew, was not his real asset. Rather it was his glib tongue
and ready smile and warm personality which made people
trust him.

Next week he would go along the river persuading the
farmers to be at the meeting and be prepared to mortgage
everything they had so they'd have money to invest in the
ditch company. He was sure he could do it. He had never
pretended to be an engineer, but had frankly admitted he
was a promoter, promoting the one thing that was vital to this
new country. You could always hire engineers, he had told
the people, but not a man who believed in what he was doing.

He dropped off to sleep, content with himself and his
future. That night he dreamed of Laura Engle.

13

Will Engle

1

Will Engle stood in the doorway of his store staring at the
crowd that was milling around under his cottonwoods. He
wondered bleakly why this couldn't have happened last
fall when he had a store full of supplies to sell. The first
ones who had come this morning had bought all the canned
goods he had left, and just a few minutes ago the last sack
of sugar had gone. Ordinarily he sold nothing on Sunday,
but already he had sold more this morning than he had any
day since he had opened the store last September.

He had nothing left except some odds and ends that
probably wouldn't sell at all. A horse collar, a singletree,
two blankets, some harness, a can of salve, and a few
other trinkets that didn't amount to anything. He had
money in his pocket for the first time in weeks, but it
wasn't enough to restock the store. He didn't have time to
start over anyhow. He just didn't have that long to live.

After the meeting was over, he'd give all the money he
had to Laura. It was small enough payment against the

money he had borrowed from her last summer, but it was all he had and the chances were he wouldn't have any more. Then a thought alarmed him. In a crowd like this there probably were some outlaws who might get the idea of holding him up, thinking he had more money than he had.

He went to the back of the room where he slept and picked up the revolver that he kept under his pillow and, returning to the door, laid the gun on the counter. The pain in his chest was worse this morning. It had been getting worse ever since that terrible day last September when he had discovered the whisky was gone and he had almost killed Charley McGivern.

To all intents and purposes he had quit living that day. Since then there had been no more big plans, no more rainbows to chase, no more dreams. He was whipped. This had been his last chance. He had known it right along, and he had bobbled it just as he had the others, first when Whit Bailey had thrown him off the claim he had staked, and second when he found that the whisky had been stolen.

The whisky would have brought men to his store. They would have bought other things and he would probably have turned his entire stock within a month. He could have restocked and he could have sold some lots and Engle City would have got off the ground before Montrose was even started.

But all of this was might-have-beens. It was too late to undo anything that was done. The pain hit him hard then and he leaned on the counter, unable to breathe for a time. One of these times a pain like that would finish him. He guessed his heart would just explode. Anyhow the doctor had told him he didn't have long. He might go today. Tomorrow. Next week.

After he left the doctor's office he went into a saloon and played poker with a crazy idea of taking some money back to Laura, but he'd lost, so he'd got drunk, hoping he'd die before he sobered up, but he didn't. He'd passed out somewhere along the road between Montrose and the store, and when he'd come to, he'd staggered on home. Laura, completely disgusted with him, had told him to go to the river and clean up and not let her see him until he had.

He sighed. Well, he couldn't blame her. He saw the

truth more plainly than he had seen it since that night in Golden when he'd come back to the wagon and found that Laura's mother had died. He remembered putting an arm around Laura and hugging her and saying, "I swear to you, Laura, that this will never happen to you. Somehow we'll change things. I won't let you go hungry all the time and freeze like this. You're going to school. You're going to be a fine lady."

He wiped a sleeve across his eyes. It came away wet. He had been an old woman lately, crying whenever he thought about those drifting years with Laura and the way he had let her mother die. It was a wonder Laura had stayed with him all this time, and an even bigger wonder she had given him the money to start this store.

He saw her walking beside Mark Manning. He hated Manning. God, how he hated the man, hated him for his courage and his ability to do things and for his wisdom. He had been right about so many things. And he hated him because Laura loved him and because he had tried to take Laura from him almost from the day he had made camp on the Gunnison. Well, it wouldn't be long until Manning could have her.

Dave Rawlins was out there, shaking hands and patting babies on the head like a politician. That was what he was, too. A good one, though, good enough to fool the farmers and even the big shots in Montrose who had money. He'd come around several times lately hinting that he was going to let Will Engle in on this irrigation project if Engle would do him a favor. He hadn't ever said what the favor was.

Engle almost laughed when we wondered what these fools would say if they knew Dave Rawlins and his partner had stolen Engle's whisky and had almost brought about a blood letting that would have made the Meeker massacre look like a tea party.

He was the only one except Laura and Rawlins himself who knew what the man was. How could people be stupid enough to trust him? But it happened all the time. Here he was, Will Engle who had never done anything worse than commit some petty theft such as stealing a chicken when he and Laura had been hungry years ago, but he had failed at everything he'd ever tried, and Rawlins, a man responsible for peddling whisky to the Indians and who could easily have been guilty of murder because of it, was riding high and handsome.

He saw Rawlins glance at his watch, then turn and start toward the store. Engle still didn't know exactly what the man had in mind. All he knew was that Rawlins was going to make him rich as soon as the ditch company was organized and had enough capital to start work.

A few months ago Engle might have been excited, but not any more. Nothing mattered now except that he live out these last few days with Laura in peace. Well, he'd let Rawlins talk and then Rawlins would go away and start the meeting and that would be the end of it.

Another savage pain shook him. He was just getting over it when Rawlins came in, saying cheerfully, "How are you this morning, Engle?" Then he seemed to realize that Engle wasn't well, and he asked anxiously, "Are you all right?"

"Sure," Engle said.

"Good. I wanted to talk to you so I'd be sure we had everything straight before the meeting. We're going to make it. I'm certain of it. We have some big men here today from both Montrose and Ouray. They're receptive to our plans, and with what the farmers can raise and my own funds, we'll have enough capital to start.

"Now my idea is to build a low dam here on your property just high enough to raise the water level so it will flow into the main canals which we'll run across your land. I'm going to suggest that the company pay you a thousand dollars for the right of way and the dam site. How does that sound, Engle? I guess you could do a hell of a lot with that much money, couldn't you? Restock your store, for instance."

Engle had been only half-listening. He had been watching Ann Collins and Lieutenant Jason Mills talk to Laura and Manning, and he had seen the anxious expression on Effie Allen's face. He thought with sudden and surprising insight that in a way he had been as bad as Effie in keeping Laura from marrying Manning. He'd never had any use for Effie, not from the moment she'd camped on the Gunnison, so, now that he thought about it that way, he guessed he didn't have much use for himself. When he died and stood up there in front of St. Peter who was looking over his record . . .

Rawlins had stopped talking. The silence ran on for a long time until he said slowly, "Engle, if you don't want to listen to what I'm saying, we'd better forget the whole deal. There are plenty of other places on this river where we can take the water, you know."

"I'm listening," Engle said wearily. "Go ahead."

"All right," Rawlins said. "Now this time you listen carefully. I told you I expected a favor from you. I think you know I'm very fond of Laura. I want to marry her. I'm going a long ways in this country, Engle. Anybody who knows me can tell you that. I can do a lot for Laura. I'll take her out of the poverty she's always lived in and I'll build her a fine home. She can call the turn, Engle. Anything she wants. All I'm asking is a chance to court her, to let her see me without the prejudice she has always had toward me. Will you persuade her to let me call on her?"

Engle had still only been half-listening, but gradually the import of Rawlins's words got through to him. He turned to look at the man, anger growing in him until it passed the point of self-control. Laura might be living in poverty, but for a man like Rawlins to presume to marry her, to have the temerity to even call on her . . . !

He had always known Rawlins was a dangerous man, but now he was too furious to think or even care. He said, his voice shaking, "Rawlins, I'd kill you before I'd let you marry her. When you start the meeting this morning, I'm going out there and tell those people that you and your partner Barney Burris stole my whisky and smuggled it onto the reservation to Colorow. I'll tell 'em it's no fault of yours that the damned Utes didn't massacre everybody who was camped back there on the line."

Rawlins' mouth dropped open from sheer shock, then a black, unreasoning fury took hold of him. His right hand swept down to the butt of his gun as he said, "You stupid little son of a bitch! Do you think for a minute I'd let you tell that to anybody?"

Engle realized then what he had done, now that it was too late. He didn't want to die from Dave Rawlins's bullet.

He might live a few more days before his heart quit and he wanted those days. He cried, "All right, I won't tell . . ."

But Rawlins revolver was relentlessly coming up. Nothing that Engle could say would stop him now. Engle made a frantic grab for the gun on the counter. He had it in his hand when Rawlins's bullet hit him in the chest and slammed him back against the counter. It didn't hurt. He'd had a far worse pain in his chest many times. Now it was just numb. He couldn't breathe. The pressure against his chest was too great.

Rawlins brushed past him. Without conscious effort Engle's finger convulsively pulled the trigger of his gun, the bullet plowing into the floor at his feet. The gun dropped from his fingers. He stumbled outside, one hand clutching his bloody shirt front, and then he fell full length on the ground.

14

Mark Manning

1

Mark marveled at the change that had taken place in Ann Collins as he watched her walk away from him and Laura, her hand resting lightly on Lieutenant Mills's arm. Mark had never seen her so happy or so attractive. Her chin was out and she walked with the assurance of a young woman who loves a man and knows she is loved in return by that man.

Laura nodded at them, smiling. "He's asked her to marry him and she said yes."

"Did she tell you?"

"No," Laura said. "I just know."

"How?"

She slapped his arm. "You think I'm going to tell you all of my womanly secrets at this stage of the game?"

"I don't keep any secrets from you."

"You don't have any womanly secrets," she said flippantly. "I'm not going to tell you everything."

Mark had turned his gaze to Effie. "Looks like she's decided to accept what she can't help."

"She's not stupid," Laura said. "Just willful." She was staring at the store. "Mark, I don't like Rawlins being in there with Pa so long."

"He won't do anything on a day like this," Mark said. "He's got too much at stake."

"I don't know," Laura said worriedly. "He stopped me on the road last Sunday when I was coming home and told me he had a big thing going. He was going to make Pa rich and he wanted to marry me."

"My rival," Mark murmured.

"I don't know what kind of pressure he thinks he can put on Pa or what Pa can put on me, but I don't like it. Mark, why do all these people trust him the way they do?"

"They don't know as much about him as we do," Mark answered. "Remember he can be very charming and persuasive when he wants to. Besides, he hooked onto the one essential in this country when he started talking about putting water . . ."

The sound of a shot from inside the store stopped him. An instant later Rawlins ran out, his gun in his hand; there was a second shot and Will Engle staggered out of the store and fell. People turned to look and stood motionless, stunned by what had happened, then Mark realized that Rawlins was racing toward his horse.

"Hold it, Rawlins," Mark yelled, and ran toward him.

Rawlins stopped when he heard Mark and whirled to face him. Men began running toward them. Rawlins stood motionless, his right arm dangling at his side, his fingers still clutching his gun. Now he raised it, his face contorted by his fury. Mark drew his revolver, for there could be no doubt of the man's intention. He had gone berserk, Mark thought, completely crazy to have gunned Will Engle down and thus in a matter of seconds thrown away all of his careful planning.

Both men fired, Rawlins getting his shot off a split second ahead of Mark. The difference was that Mark was running and therefore was a more difficult target, and Rawlins was standing still. Mark felt the bullet cut a shallow furrow along his ribs on his left side. He fired again, quickly, and knew at once the second shot was not necessary. Rawlins was knocked back by the wallop of the big slug, then he broke at every joint and fell in a collapsing sort of way like a marionette when all the strings are released at once.

Several of the women were screaming, a high, sustained sound that suddenly died.

Mark holstered his gun and strode to where Laura was holding her father's head on her lap. He didn't have long, Mark thought, as he knelt beside the man.

"Manning." Mark leaned closer to hear Engle. "You marry Laura. Make her happy. Rawlins wanted to marry her. I said I'd kill him first. I was going to tell the crowd about him and Burris stealing my whisky."

Mark glanced up to see Luke Mack standing over them. He motioned for the banker to come closer. Then he said, "When did they steal the whisky?"

"When he was camped on the Gunnison," Engle whispered. "We'd all gone to church but McGivern. Rawlins and Burris held him up and stole the whisky. They smuggled it onto the reservation and swapped it to Colorow for buckskin. That was how Colorow and his bucks got the courage to put on their war paint that last morning."

Blood bubbled at the corners of Engle's mouth. He said, "Love her, Manning. Take care of her." Then he was gone.

There was a deep silence for a moment. For a time everyone seemed too shocked by what had happened to speak or move. What Engle had said about the whisky smuggling had spread back through the crowd. There was no lower crime to those who'd had some experience with Indians.

Finally a man said, "If it hadn't been for the Army, Colorow and his bunch would have got everyone of us that was camped on the line."

And another, "By God, to think I was about to stick my money into a water company organized by that bastard."

The banker, Luke Mack, drew a long breath. "No

matter what he had done, we've got to give him credit for working on a project we've got to have, but we won't get the job done today." He nodded at a man across from him. "Morgan, fetch your wagon. We'll take Rawlins's body to town."

Lieutenant Mills helped Mark carry Will Engle's body into the store where they covered it with a blanket. When they left the building, Mark saw Laura standing motionless in front of the door, her eyes on the mesa to the west. Ann Collins had an arm around her waist, saying softly, "Go ahead and cry, Laura. You'll feel better if you do." But Laura acted as if she didn't hear.

"Jason, will you ride to town and find John Draper?" Mark said. "We'd better do the burying this afternoon, as hot as it is. He'd want to be buried here under the trees, wouldn't he, Laura?"

Laura nodded, still saying nothing. "I'll find Draper if I have to turn the town upside down," the lieutenant said. He turned to Ann. "She's going to need someone, honey. Maybe you ought to stay with her today. Tonight, too, maybe."

"Of course I will, Jason," Ann said. "I'll go tell Effie."

Mark led Laura to her cabin. She stretched out on the bed and Mark sat down beside her. She said, "I'm not as bad off as I seem. It's just that now when it's too late I wonder if I should have been a little kinder to him. I never really loved him, Mark. I just put up with him."

"It's all anyone could have done," he said. "Nobody could have been kinder than you were."

"I was just thinking about the night my mother died," Laura said. "She told me to take care of him, that he needed someone to take care of him, then she said he volunteered to fight for the Union and he was wounded in the battle of Wilson's Creek. She said he'd done one brave thing." Laura swallowed and moistened her dry lips with the tip of her tongue. "Mark, today he did another brave thing. He fought with Rawlins because Rawlins wanted to marry me. When he told Rawlins he would kill him before he'd let him marry me, he must have known he couldn't win fighting a man like that." She swallowed again. "I wonder if there aren't a lot of men who die without having done even one brave thing in their whole life.''

"You're right, Laura," he said gently. "A lot of men die without ever having done a brave thing. You can be proud of your pa."

She sighed and was silent, and Mark, watching her, knew that this was the assurance she needed.

2

They buried Will Engle late that afternoon. After John Draper led the last hymn and prayed the last prayer, he went to Laura and took both of her hands in his. He said earnestly, "It's not for me to judge my fellow men, Miss Laura. That is something only God can do, but you told me that your father was baptized when he was a boy, so I have no doubt whatever that he will share God's gift of eternal life."

"Thank you, Mr. Draper," Laura said.

The group broke up after that, the few neighbors who were there going to their homes, Effie giving Draper a ride back to the mesa in her wagon, and Ann walking off through the trees with Lieutenant Mills.

"They're getting married as soon as Jason can find a house at the post to live in," Mark said. "He told me this afternoon he thought it would be about a month."

"I think they'll be happy." Laura walked to the river bank and sat down, her back to the adobe hills on the other side of the stream. She asked in a low voice, "When, Mark?"

"The bride names the day," he said. "I've waited for you a long time. I don't want to wait any longer if I can help it."

"Tomorrow," she said. "There's no need to wait now. Pa doesn't need me any longer, but I need you, Mark. I need you so much."

"Tomorrow then,'' he said.

"Will you love me always, Mark? Even if I burn the meat for supper? Or if I give you a girl when you want a boy?"

Mark smiled. "Always, honey, no matter what."

"Do you remember that first ride we took?" she asked, "and we talked about the reservation being a land of promises? Different promises to different people?"

"I'll never forget it," he said.

They were silent for a time, Mark thinking how few of them had really worked out for the people they knew. With Will Engle it had been the big dream of a store, a saloon, and Engle City, but for him there had only been frustration and finally death. For Effie there would be loneliness again with Ann gone. The ranch on the mesa would not change that. For Ann the promise had been more than kept, for she would have her husband and her home and the babies she wanted. For John Draper it had been at least partially kept. He had his flock to whom he would preach, and soon he would have a church building. Mark did not know what sort of promise the land had given to Barney Burris and Dave Rawlins, but whatever it was, the promise had not been kept. Like Will Engle, they had found early graves.

But for Mark and Laura? The promise had been a cattle ranch on a mesa, a promise the land would keep if they wanted it to. But Mark didn't. Now he must tell her.

"There is one thing . . ." He stopped, for he knew how stupid it must seem to her to have worked so hard and then walk off because of a conscience that had been given him by his father and which would be a part of him as long as he lived.

"I know," she said. "You don't want to stay on the reservation, do you?"

He looked at her in surprise. "How did you know?"

"John Draper told me," she answered. "He said you were like Jacob who wrestled all of one night with God. He said you would wrestle with God all the time you stayed here."

"Yes, I guess I would," he said thoughtfully. "Old John is smarter than I gave him credit for." He hesitated, and then he said, "It sounds crazy to tell it, but I've been pulled two ways ever since I worked here and saw the mesa and felt it was a place where I wanted to live. I told myself I wasn't responsible for what the government did to the Utes and I might just as well have the land as anyone else. All the time I intended to come and live here, so I guess I put out the little fire in the back of my mind that said I couldn't live here when the time really came."

He took his pipe out of his pocket and filled and lighted it, then he went on, "That's why I came to the Gunnison and made the run and settled there on the mesa. Now when I go off and leave it, I'm not going to be sorry because I wanted to be close enough to you to see you all winter, and if I'd left last fall, I might have lost you. But it's crazy, Laura, being pulled one way and then the other, and having such a hard time making a decision."

"Isn't everyone that way?" she asked. "All the time this winter I've wanted to leave Pa and go to you, and I kept telling myself I would, that I didn't owe Pa anything. You see, I was afraid I'd lose you."

He took his pipe out of his mouth and grinned. "I wasn't going to be easy to lose."

"Now after what's happened," she said, "I'm glad I didn't leave Pa."

He nodded, knowing they would have happier lives because she had stayed. He said, "But the craziest of all is my feeling that the mesa is haunted by the Utes. Sometimes when I hear a cricket or a night bird or maybe a coyote, I have this crazy notion that Ouray is talking to me from his spirit land. Seems to me he keeps saying that the whites are liars, that we promised to let them live here and then we broke our promise. And that I, too, am to blame."

His pipe had gone cold in his hand again and he took his time lighting it. Finally he went on, "I don't believe the way John Draper does, about confession and baptism being the doors to Heaven and all that. It seems to me we fight evil inside ourselves and we save our souls by what we do and how we feel. So now if I do something I have a legal right to do but which I know is wrong, I've lost my soul. Do you see?"

"Yes, I see," she said softly.

"Laura, I can't stay here. A cattle ranch isn't worth it. Somewhere else, but not on the reservation. I don't know how you feel, but . . ."

"Oh Mark, I hate this valley," she said. "I thought you knew. I've hated it from the day we first saw it when we were coming down Cedar Creek. I want to live some place like along the Gunnison or up Tumitchi Creek where you see grass and a stream and trees on the hills." She paused, then threw out a hand toward the adobe hills across the river. "Those are the things that haunt me, Mark. I can't stand to look at them. Maybe it's because they're so barren that they seem symbolic of what our life would be if we stayed here."

"We'll find a place we like," he said. "Somewhere."

"Why not let John Draper have your ranch?" she asked. "He did some of the work. Maybe we ought to help Effie with her cattle, too."

He nodded, smiling. "Ouray's ghost won't keep John awake at night, and I guess Effie could use our help." He kissed her, and said, "Time I was riding. Tomorrow?"

"Tomorrow," she said.

As he rode away, he thought about his father's question: Why do men do the things they do to other men? Now for the first time in his life he realized it was a poor question. His father had not been a happy man, so he had been thinking of evil when he asked the question. But all of life was not evil. Mark had learned this since he had come to the Gunnison last August. A man must search for good if he is to balance the evil that seems to be all around him. This Mark had done. How else would he have found Laura?